HER CYBORG AWAKES

Diaspora Worlds Book One

Melisse Aires

Copyright

Table of Contents

Acknowledgements

FORMERLY TITLED **Cybot, Awakened,** with Red Rose Press.

Cover artist: Melisse Aires

Stock photos:

Canstock Photos

Pixabay

Newsletter

Please sign up to get emails of new releases and sales.
<u>sendfox.com/melisseaires</u>[1]

Blurb

TRADED TO A WARLORD'S harem as a teen, Sabralia decides to hide on the beach rather than 'entertain' her warlord's officers. When the debauchery turns into a violent coup, her docile cyborg servant turns into a warrior and steals a spaceship. He has reverted to the man he once was, and is unlike any man she's ever met. Then a failsafe shuts him down, and she must figure out how to save both of them.

Read the sexy scifi romance of Sabralia and her cyborg! Book One of the Diaspora Worlds Series.

The Diaspora Worlds Series
Her Cyborg Awakes: The one with the harem girl
Alien Blood: The one with the wilderness contest
Starwoman's Sanctuary: The one with the socialworker
Escaping Poison: The one hiding in an alien jungle
Diapora Worlds Bundle: All of them
Cyborg Security: a short story in the Diaspora Worlds

Chapter One

THE GOWN WAS EXQUISITE, an artistic creation made specifically to accentuate Sabralia's best features. She'd never looked lovelier in all her life. The finest Tanur lace, in shades of red, blue, and green, brought out the blue of her eyes and contrasted nicely with her long, dark brown hair. A low-cut neckline revealed deep cleavage, thanks to the ingenious cylifters in the gown's bodice. Alfyt the Harem master was a genius at knowing what made a woman look alluring.

Sabralia swallowed hard and tried to look pleased. Alfyt was observant and she didn't want him to notice anything odd about her behavior. Like how much she hated dressing in a translucent gown for the pleasure of the Emperor's military commanders.

"Turn around," Alfyt ordered, and she spun. The lacy gown floated, thanks to the cleverly concealed cylifters in the skirt.

"Yes. I think the sapphire and ruby jewelry will do." Alfyt looked at her with narrowed eyes and then punched sensors on his arm com. "Qy, bring lot one hundred and seventy-four."

Qy, her personal cyborg, fetched the jewelry from the Emperor's vault. Bracelets, anklets, finger and toe rings of the most delicate workmanship were fitted onto her.

"I don't like the necklace," Alfyt said. "Qy, I want you to fix her hair in an upsweep, and weave the necklace through the hair so the collar and pendant drop to her forehead." He held the necklace to her hair to demonstrate. "Yes, that will bring out her eyes and leave her cleavage unadorned. Really, it needs no adornment. And apply jeweled lashes, the permanent type so she won't have to reapply them. There won't be much time for your servant to repair your makeup during the feast days," Alfyt explained. "They will have many duties. You'll have to attend to it yourself."

Sabralia left the fitting. She sighed and paused at the doorway of the main hall to see if she could make a swift path through the Common Harem. The main hall consisted of one huge room with a high-vaulted ceiling, all in gleaming pink-veined white stone. It was filled with furniture groupings, pools, eating areas, dance and exercise areas. The community bedrooms were visible through high-arched doorways off the main hall. Cyborgs and cleaning droids moved silently around, cleaning and caring for clothing and other domestic chores. From what she could see most of the harem girls were still asleep. Good. A few women who were awake sat on the terrace overlooking the pleasure garden with its pools and lounge chairs, being waited on by staff cyborgs. Laughter and splashing floated through the high-arched doorways and windows, so there were a few in the pool. Sabralia doubted they had woken early and decided to swim. They had probably been up all night making use of the intoxicants the Main Harem was allowed to use.

Sabralia knew they envied her. She had her own suite of rooms, her own beautiful cyborg, and she was actually married to Sirn. Most of the Common Harem came from pleasure centers where they had been sex workers or dancers who caught the Emperor's eye, and they wanted a marriage contract.

Why they would want to be contracted for life to Sirn, Sabralia wasn't certain. She was a wife because it pleased his vanity to have the hereditary Queen of Coloun in his harem, and the treaty which involved her marriage was favorable to the people of Coloun. In uncertain times of war, her people had welcomed the offer from Sirn. She herself had been just a girl, barely sixteen, and she was given no choice in the matter.

Head high, eyes straight ahead on the staircase that led to her own rooms, Sabralia entered the main hall and walked swiftly to her destination.

"Hey. You. Queennie. When you going to share that cyborg with us? We could teach him a few tricks."

Sabralia didn't bother to answer. If she did, the taunting would get worse and she did not want a scene that would require the summoning of the harem cyborgs to escort her to her rooms.

As she mounted the stairs she heard the murmurs and giggles and sighed. They, at least, had friends to talk to and all sorts of games and amusements, while she had her suite of rooms and her cyborg. The other wives lived in a separate residence, but since Sirn had little use for her she'd been given rooms in the Main Harem. She wasn't one of the wives he ever summoned to please him, and she was tucked away where there would be the least fuss.

Later in her rooms on the third floor, Sabralia sat in the shade of her balcony and let the familiar sight of the aqua clear ocean soothe her. The whole idea of this upcoming banquet upset her to the point where she felt physically ill. She, Sabralia, former Queen of Coloun, legal wife to Emperor Sirn, was to be nothing more than a pleasure girl for Sirn's Commanders. It was wrong, a disgrace—and yet she had no way to refuse. Sirn's words were law here on the planet he called Sirn's Jewel. If she refused, who knew what could happen? He could cancel the trade agreement with her homeworld, turn it into a slave world, starve her people by demanding all the agricultural products Coloun could produce. He could execute her, or cast her out on the glidepath of some cesspool of a spaceport.

"Mistress, you have a message." Qy handed her the small com. She held it for a moment, not wanting to read the message from Alfyt. "It is a reminder about the Feast."

With a soft sigh she played the message.

"The Emperor's Harem will arrive in their feasting garb an hour before the festivities, to be inspected by Alfyt before the Emperor arrives with his guests. Instruct your cyborgs to decorate your hair and skin for a most formal event." She shivered, feeling suddenly cold, and squeezed her eyes shut. Sirn cared not at all about his harem; they were just tools for his use.

"Does something trouble you, Mistress?"

She glanced at Qy. All the cyborgs were spies; it was built into their programming. They recorded and uploaded all harem conversations during their nightly maintenance, and a sophisticated program checked all contents for signs of trouble, especially for disloyalty to the Emperor. Disciplinary actions followed.

"No. I am just thinking about how I want my hair arranged for the feast."

"I will pull the front of your hair high and wind into decorative curls, to give you some height, and we can leave long curls down the back. I will entwine the necklace through the curls."

"Yes. It is to be most formal."

Qy was exceptional at his job of decorating Sabralia so she looked her best, as were all of the cyborgs of the Harem. Her coloring was a rather duller copy of his own, she thought, observing him move about her quarters doing his chores. Where his hair was blue-black, hers was dark brown; where his eyes were pale sky blue, hers were a muddy blue gray. His skin was naturally bronze, hers very pale with a tracery of blue veins.

She was round and sturdy, with big eyes, big lips, big breasts and hips. There was nothing delicate or elegant about her, but Qy would give her the illusion of beauty. She had been plump all her life, which was not at all the fashion here in the Harem full of lithe dancers, and the inactivity in her life made her curves even fuller. So she was diligent about getting some exercise every day.

HER GOWN ARRIVED IN triplicate, so she could wear a fresh gown each day of the feast and be easily recognized by the Commanders who fancied her. Too bad the beauty was all for the enjoyment of men who would just use her. Rape her.

Sabralia couldn't breathe. She had to get outside. "Come, let us walk by the sea. I would like to splash a little," she said when Qy finished with her raiment. "It is a lovely day." She made her voice deliberately cheerful. If she didn't get outside for a while she was afraid she would break down into tears, and that would be reported to Alfyt.

Down by the water she could think—think of a way to avoid being raped by the Emperor's finest. And if she cried a few tears, the ocean water would disguise it. She slipped into a simple swim tunic and thin leggings and Qy accompanied her down her private stairs to the sandy beach.

The palace was on a hill overlooking a wide bay. Long stretches of white sand contrasted with the pristine blue green waters of the sea. This was a beautiful world, with a warm climate and abundant forests and meadows. It would be an ideal agricultural world, but Sirn had not opened it to colonists, and none of the native life forms were sentient. Sirn only used it for military installations and his palace. Sirn held hunting parties now and then, and the dangerous beasts had been removed from the palace and spaceport area. The women of the Common Harem did not have access to this section of beach because it stretched close to the spaceport, and Sirn did not want them distracting his men. But she had been deemed not a security risk to the spaceport. She'd been married to Sirn since her teen years and had no military or spacecraft education, nor was she flirtatious as far as their records indicated.

A wonderful, scary idea came to her as she floated, letting a gentle wave glide her to shore. The beach! That was the answer!

Alfyt and the cyborgs would be tremendously busy during the feast. She would tell Qy to prepare a luxurious pallet, with food and drink, at her special place on the beach, because one of the Commanders wanted to be entertained outdoors, by the sea. Later she would lie and tell Qy her man had visited while Qy was at his nightly maintenance—her mind raced with the plan. She would hide on the beach until the feast ended and the Commanders left.

Leaving the water, Sabralia took off down the beach thinking of a small cove near the forest, well out of sight of the palace. The place had a small area of grass fronting the woods, which were just a short upward trail above the beach. She'd had picnics here before, enjoying the view of the beach. Wildflowers grew year round in the meadow and the floral scents mingled with the fresh breezes from the sea, making it even more pleasant. The forest behind it stretched a long way, all the way to Sirn's Spaceport.

"I love this spot, Qy," she said when they reached it. "It is my favorite little cove, with the trees. Let us come here for lunch tomorrow."

"Yes, Mistress."

She knew Qy would recall the location at any time she mentioned her favorite cove. Cyborgs were good that way.

The morning of the feast, Sabralia woke in Qy's arms. She had trained Qy to hold her from the time he returned to her room from his nightly maintenance, until she woke. He was a machine, of course, but his body was a man's, fit and smooth skinned. She enjoyed the sensation of his warm smooth flesh next to her every night. The touching normally helped a little, with the loneliness. But this morning there was no comfort in his arms. Tonight was the feast.

Qy gave her an engaging smile. When he smiled like that he looked so warm and human. His eyes seemed to glow with sky blue light. With his black curls tousled and covering most of the plate that curved over one temple and ear, Sabralia could almost forget he was a cyborg. She suspected that the human body Qy had been fashioned from had been a genetically engineered human, a Puregen. Emperor Sirn had been pushing his invasion into the Puregen Systems for years, anxious to gain their wealth and technology. Most of the cyborgs at the palace seemed to come from that stock. Under their appliances, they were all startlingly handsome.

"Good morning, my love," he said in his rich, warm tone. "Would you like me to feed you your breakfast? Or would you like to bathe first?"

Her stomach was a tight knot of pain. "I am not hungry yet. I would like to bathe."

"Would you like me to bathe with you?"

Sabralia hesitated for just a moment. Qy was trained to either bathe her quickly and efficiently, or to get into the bathing pool with her. Baths with him in the pool were far more intimate. Sabralia's face turned hot. She wanted the intimate bath, wanted to feel his hard body naked against hers...and maybe it would help calm her down about the Feast. Or perhaps it would be her last pleasurable moment for a long time.

Most of the harem cyborgs were used for sex. Sabralia thought it was disrespectful to the men they had once been, before their brains had been replaced by processors. Sometimes though, she opted for a long, slow bath, where QY would wash every inch of her skin.

"Bathe with me, Qy."

"Yes, Mistress." Without hesitation, he slid off his wrap shirt and loose trousers, revealing his golden, muscular body, lithe and perfect. Broad of shoulder, slim of hip, he only had cyborg hardware on his forearms, one thigh, and just above one side, stretching back to his spine. If she put her arms around him just right she could feel flesh, nothing but smooth flesh, covering taut muscle. His sex was surrounded by a riot of shiny black curls, and there was a small sprinkling of soft black hair drawing a line up his torso, and a light growth of hair on his chest. She could have his hair removed, of course, but she liked the contrast of black hair and golden skin. She liked how the silky hair on his chest felt under her fingers or against her cheek when she snuggled him at night. His penis was long and flaccid. He did not get aroused like a human man. It was something the Harem girls had to manipulate and teach their bots.

Qy would breathtaking like that, it was tempting to have him for sexual pleasures, but the cyborg had to be taught every move, just like they had to be taught everything else. The idea of teaching Qy how to have sex, how to pleasure her that intimately, was daunting. It had taken a long time to teach him to use caressing strokes when he bathed her, and his deep kisses had only recently become less mechanical.

Plus Sabralia new how vulnerable she was from loneliness. What if she developed stronger feelings for her servant, only to have him replaced by another? Often the servants were evaluated and moved to military installations to perform more complex tasks. Someday they would take Qy, and she didn't need to add to her grief.

Qy gently disrobed her and helped her into the steaming pool, scented with sweet Bellflowers from her homeworld. He slid in beside her and they sank into the warm water. She sat between his open legs. His large hands slid gently up her arms and she shivered with anticipation. This morning she would...indulge. She didn't, not very often, because her emotions for Qy seemed overwhelming then, and he was only a cyborg. He could never be a true lover. His brain no longer functioned like a human's; he had no personality or thoughts. As a contract wife in the harem, one that didn't hold Emperor Sirn's affections, she was not popular, nor was she ever called to the Emperor's bed. The women of the harem...few could be trusted. So many curried favor and attention, hoping their name would get back to the Emperor, or even to Alfyt, the harem Master. She couldn't trust them, so Sabralia kept to herself, her only constant companion Qy. But she knew it would be wrong and emotionally dangerous to let her emotions grow for a cyborg.

With his hands massaging her shoulders she could pretend he was more than a cyborg, for a short while, and forget about the upcoming feast. Who knew what would happen at the feast. Rape. She shivered despite the hot water.

"I would like a full massage this morning."

"Wonderful. I love to touch you everywhere." He replied with the phrase she taught him. His hands soon left her shoulders and rubbed down to her lower back, pressing and circling with strong fingers. His touch seemed to go deep inside her body, almost removing the unpleasant tightness within her.

He cleaned her breasts with slick fragrant cleanser. She had never taught him to play with her nipples, but his massaging touch brushed them constantly, sending tingles of pleasure through her body. She felt the deep tension melt way.

"It is time for you to lean on the side, Sabralia." She kneeled, resting her head on her arms on the side of the pool. Qy's hand slid to her buttocks, squeezing and stroking in a deep massage, and she melted in bliss. Heat flooded through her and she could feel herself get wet. His hands slid down her legs, massaging her thighs, her calves. He spent much time on her feet, rubbing each toe in a circular motion. Then he turned her around and massaged up the front of her legs.

"The nozzle now? Or kissing?" His voice was low, seductive, like she had taught him.

"Kissing."

Qy was not the best of kissers, not as she remembered kissing boys in her youth. His movements were mechanical, and she found she enjoyed the kissing more if she was already aroused. Knowing that kissing her did not give him pleasure or arousal took much of the pleasure away for her.

They kissed for short while, then she murmured, "The nozzle."

"Yes." He slid a water nozzle between her legs. She wrapped her arms about his neck and they kissed, while he applied the stream of water to her clit. She came with a shudder, and then buried her face in his neck, crying for things she couldn't have, for the life she was trapped in.

"I will wash your hair now, Mistress." Qy proceeded to cleanse and rinse her with clear water, while she let tears stream down her face. She never felt lonelier than after she came in the arms of her cyborg. He wasn't really there with her, had no ability for emotional communion...her life was empty, unless she pretended.

But the tension was gone, for a moment. Did she really dare to hide on the beach?

She ate a small breakfast, but didn't feel like doing anything. Qy sat with her on the divan on the balcony overlooking the sea, and they watched the waves. She closed her eyes after a while, though sleeping was no real solution.

Chapter Two

SABRALIA DRESSED CAREFULLY in her new gown. The colors made her skin look whiter and her eyes a mysterious dark blue. Qy did her hair in an elaborate upsweep, but showed her several simple but elegant styles she could do herself if her hair got mussed while he was busy.

Bile rolled up her throat at the thought of activities that would muss her hair.

The festivities began with a meal, followed by a series of performances, some from the Harem, and others from professional troupes and musicians hired for the occasion. Emperor Sirn sat in a shielded box overlooking the stage. Sabralia sat near the side aisle, where she could slip away, next to several older women, contract wives like herself. Only they had children by Sirn, and so they would retire to their quarters after the meal, safe from the officers. Other harem women were giggling and whispering, already flirting with the officers, who were dressed alike in their white and orange formal uniforms. The officers looked hard, like men who got what they wanted, no matter what. Sabralia shivered and tried to avoid any eye contact with them. Lucky for her, many of the harem women were working hard to be visible and noticed by the men. Sabralia slid down in her seat and watched the extravagant program.

She slipped out to the retiring room before the program was over and used her com to call for Qy to come check her hair. While she waited for him she pulled on a section of her gown and caused a small tear. Now she had an excuse to go up to her rooms.

Qy came to inspect her hair and makeup, which was fine. It was now or never. She took a steadying breath. "Qy, please take our beach equipment to the small cove at the beach I enjoy so much. I have met a gentleman who would enjoy an outdoor evening of relaxation. Provide all manner of refreshments and a comfortable pallet with blankets."

"Yes, Mistress." Qy left to do his business.

Heart in her throat, she slipped up a side stair to her rooms. She thought about changing out of her gown but had no way to explain the change if she was caught, so she just switched her shoes for beach sandals and slipped down the stairs from her balcony to the sand.

The beach was unfamiliar in the dark, and she was jumpy, afraid she would run into someone. A man with a hard face and harsh, painful hands. But she found the cove without incident and sat on the still warm sand to wait for Qy.

"Mistress, I am here." Qy announced his presence. He pulled a small float with a large basket filled with wine, fruit drinks, and an array of delicate food stuffs in a cooler. He set up a large soft pallet with silken pillows near a small brazier, which danced with a flame. It was a lovely romantic setting, one she could imagine lovers sharing, which made her feel immeasurably sad.

"Wonderful. My gentleman is coming along in a short while. He wished to be near the sea, in fresh air. Keep our location a secret, also. We wish to have our privacy. You may return after your nightly maintenance." She helped herself to a fruit drink, then wrapped herself in a blanket and rested on the cushioned pallet.

"Yes, Mistress." Qy left, taking the cart with him, and she knew he would obey her words. And if she needed him she could summon him via her com. There was nothing to do except stay alert in case someone came down the beach. Sabralia turned down the brazier flame until it was as small as a candle. It was dark, and the only sounds were night birds and the sound of the sea. She helped herself to the food and drink, and even emptied a bottle of wine into the sea after pouring it into two glasses, which she also poured out. It would look like her companion had come, had food and drink, if Qy was questioned. Eventually she leaned back against the cushions and dozed. She awoke when Qy returned.

"I will be sleeping here tonight, Qy. My gentleman spoke of returning here at a later time."

"Yes, Mistress."

She insisted he get under the covers with her. She didn't think cyborgs felt cold, but she felt safer with him beside her. "Wake me if anyone comes, please."

It was a long night, but quiet. No revelers came down the beach.

Qy was with her when she woke in the morning. She lied, in case the cyborgs were reporting their ladies' activities. "While you were at maintenance, my gentleman visited me. He was quite pleased with our comfortable situation, and would like me to remain here, awaiting his visits. Can you bring more refreshments and drinks?"

Qy questioned nothing, and did her bidding. That afternoon, Sabralia paddled for a short time in the sea, then dressed in one of the other sheer gowns designed for the festivities. Qy did not join her in the water. His appliances and muscular physique made him sink like a stone, and he did need oxygen for his flesh parts. She wished she had different clothing, but if she were to be caught, at least her gown fit with her outdoor lover story. Qy fixed her hair, but after he left she put the jewels away in an embroidered pocket that held her cosmetics, and did her hair into a simple braid. She would have to account for the jewelry later.

"What is happening in the palace, Qy?" she asked later.

"The kitchen is very busy supplying food and drink. Medical has also been busy since so many have used too many intoxicants. Some of the harem and a few of the officers had minor injuries in fights."

"Are my rooms all right?" The distasteful thought of strange couples using her rooms for dalliance suddenly occurred to her.

"Yes, Mistress. I locked your rooms."

"Good. But it does sound like the officers are having a fine time."

"Yes, Mistress, a fine time," Qy echoed.

Qy rested with her on the blankets that night until it was time for his maintenance. Sabralia figured she would again tell him the soldier visited her while he was gone, since a cyborg would not be suspicious, but Qy came back not long after leaving.

"Qy, why aren't you at maintenance?" Had Alfyt sent him for her? Her heart leaped to an uncomfortable speed.

"The doors were locked, Mistress. I could not get into the maintenance room. I went into the main hallway, to take a different door, but there was much confusion."

"What do you mean?"

"Would you like to hear the recording?"

"Yes."

Qy pressed his leg implant. Weapon blasts, shouting, and screaming filled the night. The sounds of violence. Dread clutched at her gut and suddenly the balmy breeze felt cold.

"It did not look safe, Mistress."

"Yes... I'm sure you are right." Her heart pounded so hard she felt dizzy.

There is some type of ambush in the palace!

"I think we should move our bedding deeper into the woods, in case the unrest comes closer," she said. She wanted to hide, to be safe.

"Yes, Mistress."

They moved up the steep hillside into the woods, where the canopy of the trees blocked the light of the stars, and found a small clearing. It was frightening in the dark. Qy brought the brazier and the food and drink basket after leaving her briefly. She dozed fitfully in his arms, too scared of soldiers to turn on the brazier.

In the morning, Qy returned to the palace. Sabralia waited nervously from a spot in the trees where she could watch the beach. He returned some time later with food stuffs.

"Have things calmed down there?" she asked.

"They are not running on schedule," he replied. "The kitchen was empty, and none of the cyborgs were cooking. I gathered breakfast and luncheon for you, Mistress. I did not go into the main rooms, just like you instructed. The maintenance room was still locked."

She did not know what to think. "Very good, Qy."

Sabralia spent a nervous day in the woods, not daring to go down to the beach for a swim. Qy sat on a small rise some distance away, watching the beach and distant palace. A few ships blasted into orbit from the spaceport on the far side of the forest, the roar filling the woods and making her heart thunder. *What is happening?*

Towards evening they saw smoke rising, either on the far side of the palace or one of the outbuildings just beyond.

"Should I investigate?" Qy asked. "Alfyt has not summoned me for duty all day."

"No, Qy, it looks like more unrest. Alfyt must have other duties in an emergency. I think you should remain with me. Perhaps my soldier will come and tell us what is happening."

"Yes, Mistress."

The sun went down. The smell of smoke was stronger for a while, until the cool evening breeze from the sea pushed the smoke farther away. Sabralia wondered what was happening to the women—were they safe? Were they dead? None had come along the beach. Exhausted, she finally slept, wrapped in the blankets and her cyborg's arms.

KAISTRIL DREAMED. A woman was in his arms...his Mistress Sabralia, with her dark hair, dark blue eyes, and white soft skin. His cock roared into hardness. He tightened his arms around the woman, pulling her closer...she was so sweet, smelling of flowers, her soft bottom cradled his straining member...

Something is wrong. His eyes snapped open in a starless night and he sat up so fast he swayed, dizzy. They were on a cushioned pallet in thick woods. A body was pressed tight against him and he knew it was his Mistress Sabralia. They were hiding from...unrest.

Something is wrong.

My name is Kaistril.

No! I am Qy, in service to my mistress.

He couldn't remember...but Kaistril seemed right.

He shook his head to try and clear his confusion. The air reeked of smoke. The fire, soldiers, danger, weapons... His head ached, as did his stomach. He was thirsty. He reached into Sabralia's food basket and got a fruit drink, which helped a little, but his mind was still clouded.

They were in the woods...a fire at the palace...

Something is wrong.

Breathe deeply, calm yourself, a voice he recognized as being from his past told him. He closed his eyes and breathed in through his nose and out through his mouth, concentrating.

There was a sound. It was important. He listened.

Far away, so far away, he could only feel the vibrations through the earth—death! He slid off the pillows onto the forest floor and placed his palms on the ground—

—The Strafe, attacking his Tier, the entire contingent in their observation units, dying. Burning, blinding white flashes, men falling dead in an instant, dead bodies everywhere...

He knew it well. It had killed his men. The Strafe was coming!

"Wake. Wake!" He hauled the sleeping woman into his arms. "We need to get down to the beach, to one of the caves!"

A timer went off in his brain, the timer he was to obey, for his nightly maintenance. He groaned with confusion .

No—the caves! He threw the queen over his shoulder with her blankets over her, and loped toward the beach, ignoring her protests and squirms. She was round and soft, not strong, not a warrior woman, and he was able to subdue her struggles easily without harming her. In the far distance the Strafe slashed through the air, lighting the way with its killing white light, and the woman screamed in shock, her whole body going tight.

"Underground. The Strafe," he grunted. She probably had no idea what the Strafe was. But he knew. He remembered. Fierce triumph filled him. He remembered, and they would not kill this warrior, or his queen.

"What's wrong?" she cried.

The soft voice of his mistress sent a shiver down his spine. His body was still hard, clamoring for her touch, despite the raging light. The danger, the excitement flooding his body, his memories, the woman in his arms. He paused for a moment, suddenly overwhelmed with confusion.

The Strafe moved closer so its individual tines of killing light were visible.

"We need to get to one of the tidal caves. The Strafe will kill us."

"The Strafe." Comprehension colored her words. He sat her down, pulled the blanket from her face, then grabbed her hand, and they raced down the beach.

Kaistril found the section of beach with shallow caves. They'd explored them before, collecting shells. Once inside, he shoved her against the back wall of the cave and covered her body with his own.

"The Strafe doesn't go through soil. We might live if we..." His words trailed off. She was staring at him, mouth agape, eyes huge and dark in the night.

"You are different." His mistress sounded faint.

"Yes. There is no time. Close your eyes," he said. "The light can damage your vision." He pulled the blanket over them, holding it cupped to her eyes with one hand while he did the same for his own eyes. Kaistril listened carefully but could hear nothing now except their breathing, heavy with fear. The Strafe was concentrating on populated areas, though it would eventually sweep outlying areas for strays.

Bright, deadly tines stroked the beach and suddenly clashed around them, lighting even their closed, blanket-covered eyes. They sank to the ground as the light sizzled just a few feet from them, close enough they could feel its strange heat. It disappeared, though they could still hear it.

Kaistril ran out of their shelter. The Strafe had returned to the Palace area. "Come on. It has gone straight back to the city. This is our chance!"

He grabbed her by the hand and ran up the beach, dragging her along.

"Qy, where are we going?" she wailed.

He paused for a split second, then continued pulling her along.

"Staying alive is the plan," was all he said. No need to tell her it's a gamble. Soon the Harvesters will be here to kill those that remain alive...

Her breath was ragged and her legs refused to pull her any further along the beach. Kaistril threw her over his shoulder with a grunt. She was no warrior.

"Almost there, I think." He cut through the woods, and was soon parallel to the fence surrounding Sirn's spaceport. Eventually they came through the woods to a paved road and an open gate with guard towers. There were no guards.

Kaistril set her on her feet but again grabbed her hand.

"We want to find the smaller spacecrafts," he said as they passed Sirn's mid-grade war ships that most of the officer's arrived in. Sirn's largest ships did not make landing, of course, but stayed in space.

Chapter Three

THERE WERE BODIES LYING around. Sabralia moaned and averted her eyes, but Qy seemed quite interested and looked at them carefully.

"Strafe kills," he said.

Farther on they saw a body in gaudy civilian clothes, not a uniform.

Qy dropped her hand and ran to it. "Yes." Fierce triumph colored the word. "This is perfect." A hard smile, an expression she'd never seen before on Qy, flashed over his face. He dug through the clothing and yanked the bright red and blue jacket off the deceased.

"That's Alfyt!" She suddenly recognized the head of the Harem and of the cyborgs.

"Yes. Could it be more perfect?" Qy tossed the jacket over her shoulders and she squealed.

"He died of the Strafe, not some disease, and just moments ago. And you need to cover up. That transparent dress is distracting."

She gaped at him. *Distracting? He'd seen her naked hundreds of times.*

Qy turned away, pulled off Alfyt's arm com and inspected it. Then he grabbed Alfyt's bags, and headed toward a spaceship that was just a few yards away.

"Come on!" He yelled at her impatiently while she just stared at him. "Alfyt has the access code!"

What had happened to Qy? Could he have his memories back, of the man he once was? Was that even possible? Was this some type of survival programming at work? Sabralia didn't know what to think or do. But she didn't want to stay here, alone. She ran after him. They climbed up the service ladder to a small door. Qy beamed the code to the ship and the door popped open. The ship was luxurious and Sabralia gaped at it while Qy rummaged in a locker.

Qy shoved a garment and helmet at her. "Get this on and strap in. Make sure the tube is at your lips."

She nodded. She'd used a spacer suit once before, when she left her homeworld to join the harem. She pulled on the vacuum safe suit and sat next to him at the control console. He started the ship and then toddled it around the space landing.

"What are you doing?"

"Finding the fuel station. We're low."

He found it, and got out to fuel up. "See if there is food. Hopefully it is stocked and we won't have to make another stop."

While golden sludge slid down clear tubes to the fuel hold, she found a pantry and kitchen area. It was full of food, including many luxurious things. This ship must belong to someone important. Maybe even Sirn, himself. The furnishings were lovely—there was a white and peach bathing area and a sleep area with a large, beautifully covered bed.

"There's lots of food," she told him when he climbed back inside.

"Good. Grab me something to eat and a drink. Kaf, if they have it. It helps me concentrate. You might want to wait to eat, though, until we are off-world, in case your stomach reacts to take off. We have a little time, the sensors show the Strafe is miles away."

Sabralia found filled pocket breads, which were in self-heating wraps, and several drinks. She watched in amazement as Qy devoured the sandwiches and gulped down three drinks. She did not feel the least bit hungry. Her stomach was tight with nerves.

"I didn't know cyborgs could eat," she said, feeling faint. What was happening to Qy? His facial expression was different. More animated, somehow, with expressions she'd never seen on his perfect features. While he ate he turned on various ship systems and scanners.

He looked at her for a moment, then shook his head. "We'll have time to talk after we get away." He flipped down her mask and slid the connection, sealing her in, then did the same for himself.

"Let's see what she's got." He closed the hull view panels, blasted the engines, and they shot into the atmosphere.

Sabralia saw the Strafe on his scanview, coming down from somewhere higher above them. She knew it was a space-based weapon. Qy elevated the ship and headed straight for it.

"What are you doing?" she yelped.

"Trust me. This is how we get off-world undetected."

"How we get off-world undetected?" Panic rose and so did her voice.

"I know a way. Risky, but workable."

"How risky?"

"Considering our chances of staying alive here are about zero percent, I think we don't have many options. Now hush. I need to concentrate."

"Oh no," she moaned as he positioned the ship parallel to the Strafe. She could hear the deadly thrum and throb of the energy beam.

"Sweet! A chameleon hull. We look like whatever we are next to."

Qy was almost grinning, and his eyes as they looked at the screen held an intent expression she'd never seen before. She swallowed down a rush of bile. Had his circuits gotten scrambled or something? Was this some type of survival programming? Was he taking her into battle?

"I-I'm not sure we should do this."

"I'm sure. You're going to have to trust that I know best here."

Her cyborg knew best? But they couldn't think or reason, not really. Could they?

"Qy, maybe—"

"—Sabra, we are going up hard and fast. You will probably pass out, but you will be all right. Make sure the air piece is in your mouth. Now."

She nodded, tears of fear and shock streaming down her face, and positioned the tube in her mouth while he fastened his own mask. It can't be healthy to be this afraid...

The speed of their ascent crushed her into her seat, and soon all went black.

Sabralia woke up in a soft bed, covered with silky, warm covers. A delicious aroma of a hot meal filled the room. She was not wearing the spacer suit, though Alfyt's jacket still covered her gown. She climbed out of bed and noticed right away that they were in light grav. She had to move with care so she wouldn't careen into things.

Qy was standing in the kitchen area, attending a meal. He was wearing just a thin pair of spacer knit leggings, no shirt, and high soft spacer boots. Somehow he'd removed the implant on his torso, and the one on his temple. Neat newskins covered the wounds left by the implants. She saw another newskin on one arm.

"What happened to your implants?" Her voice was hoarse.

"While you were sleeping I took them off."

"Is that safe?"

"Yes, we take them off frequently for maintenance." His arm and leg implants remained. The thigh implant showed clearly under the thin knit.

He saw her glance. "The arm and leg implants are information systems. They come in handy."

She nodded. She couldn't think of anything to say. It was as if her thoughts were frozen.

It finally dawned on her that they were not moving. There was no sound of the ship's engines. "Where are we?" The view screen was dark, and the pilot section was dimly lit.

"Hidden on a chunk of rock. You slept for a long time, nearly twelve hours. I have coordinates set, but I want to rest and eat. I need to remove a tracer, which is a technical chore. I want to take it off after a good sleep. Until then, the magnetic aspect of this rock will conceal us. Once the tracer is off we'll be virtually undetectable. We can get safely away."

"Are we safe now? We got away?"

"Oh yes. The sentinels in orbit could not distinguish us from the Strafe. We jumped orbit with no problems at all."

It seemed impossible they could be safe after the events of the past few days. Sabralia sat down, and hid her shaking hands from Qy.

"The tracer works when we are moving, so with our engines powered down we're good."

Cyborgs didn't sleep or eat, and Qy never carried on conversations, though he did answer questions. She watched his every move.

"Where are we going?"

"Katherine Hub. I calculated and we have enough fuel. Stinsen Hub is actually closer, and anyone else fleeing the coup will probably go there. But I did some careful calculations and we can make it to Katherine on the fuel we have. There are a few sub stations out there where we could buy more fuel, but I wouldn't trust any of them. I shut down several unneeded systems, including Life Support on the utility level. So don't go down there."

"I don't know where that is."

"Lower level." Qy waved toward a door. He stirred vigorously, then spooned food onto two gilt platters.

"Maintenance systems are down there, they probably won't be needed during our trip. If they are I can either wear a suit or reset the Life Support." He set a platter and some utensils in front of her. "From Katherine Hub we will have time to decide what to do."

"You know how to calculate fuel, Qy?" Sabralia asked, the tension in her body so tight pain shot through her neck. This was not the cyborg she knew, who had to be taught every little thing and given orders.

"And what have you done with your hair?" Her voice was getting high and squeaky again.

His hair, those long glossy curls, had been divided into locks of tightly matted hair that hung in a wild mass to his shoulders, and the front of his hair was pulled back into a knot at the back of his head, almost covering the section where the temple implant had been. He looked barbaric and his face somehow looked harsher, more masculine. Part of that was his expression. His face was no longer bland and emotionless. There was no slackness in his mouth now.

Qy turned to her and slid those pale blue eyes up and down her body, a gaze the cyborg had certainly never used before. "Pretty curls were fine for the maidservant, my lady. But now I am once again a warrior. I wear a warrior's hair. My Tier wears their hair in this style as a sign of camaraderie."

His eyes slid over her once more, pausing on her breasts, which showed because the jacket hung open. She swallowed nervously and yanked the jacket over her, but her nipples hardened as though there was a chill.

"You remember your past?"

"Two nights without the maintenance removed the cyborg drugs from my system. I believe my memory returned fully when I heard the Strafe. My Tier fell to the Strafe." He turned away abruptly.

Qy was a cyborg name. "Wh-what should I call you?" She pushed the platter away, unable to choke down food. Qy took it and put it in a food keeper.

"My name is Kaistril. Go bathe. You will feel much better after you bathe and eat a real meal. There are spacer knits in the cupboard."

Kaistril? Could it be? I thought cyborgs were made from human remains. How could he have a memory? Sabralia watched him for a moment, confused. Alfyt had told her they had no memories because they were truly dead before they were processed. But in just this short time, he looked so different than Qy, even though he had the same face and body. He talked different. He was a man, not a cyborg.

Sabralia fled to the bathing room and just stood for a moment. Taking her clothing off made her feel exposed. He's not my cyborg anymore, he's a stranger. She locked the door. In the past she daydreamed about her cyborg changing into a man, a gentle, courtly man, who was refined, attentive. One who played a lute and recited love poems.

Kaistril did not seem to be like the man she daydreamed about. He seemed more intense. More everything. Commanding...dangerous...

She bathed in a water shower, though the luxurious bath had other options. Her skin was covered with sand from the beach, and dried sweat from their escape.

The spacer knits were soft and thin, and pale blue gray in color. Spacer knits were specially made to be resistant to any form of dirt or bacteria, and were healthy for the wearer's skin in the artificial environment of a spacecraft. The knits were able to adjust to body temperature, to keep body heat stable, and they stretched for an extremely comfortable fit. She was glad to get out of the sheer dress, which was never warm enough. She recognized a hygenie and stuffed the gown inside. While she didn't intend to wear it again, there was no point in leaving it around dirty. The cupboard held high sock-like boots, like the ones Qy wore, that fitted themselves to her foot size, and made the ship's gravity more normal for movement.

Sabralia dried her hair by herself for the first time in years. Qy always did her hair. But now he was Kaistril. A warrior, he said. Was he a good man? He was a good warrior, that much she could tell. But how did he treat women? Like walking pleasure centers? Like slaves? Was he rough? Did she escape the Feast for nothing?

Could she bear it if her loyal cyborg turned out to be a cruel man?

Sabralia walked out to the main area and Kaistril raised his head from the platter he was loading with food. He looked at her...and looked at her some more, eyes roving up and down her body.

"What's wrong?" He'd seen her naked daily, but she suddenly felt self-conscious.

"Nothing is wrong. The knits are thin. I can see your lips."

She raised a hand to her mouth, frowning a little.

"Not those lips."

Her eyes opened wide. *Did he mean...?*

He was smirking. *Yes he did!*

Chapter Four

SABRALIA FLED BACK to the bedroom and threw on Alfyt's coat. Heart pounding, she wondered if she should lock herself in the bath. He was every bit as crude as she'd imagined Sirn's Officers. And now she was stuck here alone with him.

After a while, Qy came into the doorway. "Come eat," he said.

"I'm not very hungry, thank you," she replied.

Qy came further into the room and she watched him warily. "I should not have said that," he said. "I rarely spend time with gentle women, and the women I know are not easily offended."

She nodded. For some reason, speaking was difficult around this new Qy.

Her food was on the small table when she came out, and Qy was plowing through a plateful. She sat gingerly on the chair.

Qy flicked a glance at Sabralia. "You have nothing to fear from me. I will not rape you. I am not one of Sirn's lawless men."

Sabralia had no idea how to answer that, but it did put one of her fears to rest. A little. She ate a bite of the meal he'd prepared, some type of creamy meat and pasta. "It is good," Sabralia said, somewhat surprised.

"I like to eat, so I learned to cook when I was a schoolboy in New Prague."

"You are from New Prague? Where is that?"

"It is on the edge of the Puregen Systems, where Sirn is concentrating his moves."

She'd thought he might be Puregen, a genetically altered, lab-created human. He had that perfect face and body, and his eyes were a rare sky blue. "You are Puregen?"

"Yes, but my homeworld does not have a Puregen constitution."

She looked at him blankly. "I didn't know there were Puregen constitutions."

He grinned. "That means that non-Puregen humans can hold citizenship. On Puregen constitution worlds, only Puregens can be citizens."

"Oh." Sabralia felt stupid. Her schooling had ended at age sixteen with her marriage, and the harem did not get current news of the War.

"You are from Coloun, correct?" he asked.

"Yes. It is an agricultural world that supplies Sirn's forces. Not Puregen. Of Terran descent."

"So is New Prague. Settled about five generations ago." She nodded. "Coulon was settled in the same Diaspora."

Qy helped himself to more food. "I think Sirn may be dead. You might be a widow, little queen." His look was intense, and she floundered around, trying to think of why he would care about her widowhood.

"How did you come to marry Sirn, anyway?"

"I was married as part of a treaty. We—my cousin was my guardian—thought it would be better for our planet. Our weaponry was far out-classed by Sirn. We had no chance against him."

"Why didn't you live in the Palace of the Wives?"

"I didn't get pregnant with Sirn's child, so I lost favor right away. I must have offended him in some way...I don't know. I doubt he remembers my name. I will not mourn him." She looked down at her plate, finding the intense way Qy looked at her disconcerting.

"Good." Qy stood and moved to her side. "If he is dead I will have you declared a citizen of New Prague and so you can divorce him, since he is not recognized as a citizen. And he is an enemy of my homeworld."

"You can't do that."

He grinned. "Can too. I'll copy you out our laws. I'm the captain of this ship—it is mine by spoil of war. In our laws, that is like being a judge and a governor. Once we get to New Prague, I can declare you a citizen." His grin deepened and she was struck by the difference in his smile compared to Qy's sweet, gentle one. "Then you would be a free woman. Free to be with me. If you choose."

Hot blood rushed to her face. She ducked her head and pushed food around on her plate. "Wh-what do you mean, Qy?"

"Kaistril is my name. I mean we will be alone on this ship for several weeks. We could pleasure each other."

Her fork clattered onto the plate with a clank. She shoved from the table to flee to the bathing area where she could lock the door. Qy—no, Kaistril, because Qy would never intimidate her—blocked her way.

Steely hands gripped her upper arms. She struggled against him, but found his strength too much.

"I told you I was not one of Sirn's lawless rapists. I have no intention or desire to hurt you. You are safe here." His lips curved slightly. "Or, at least, as safe as I am out here alone in space in the middle of a war." They stood in silence for a moment, bodies lightly touching. She couldn't halt her rapid breathing that brought her breasts up against his hard chest. He let her go, removed his utensils from the table, and took them to the hygenie. "Finish your meal."

She stood, undecided for a moment. But what real defense did she have if he was one of the lawless men, if he...?

Finally, she slid back into her chair.

"Tomorrow I will remove the tracer from this ship. In three days the orbit of this rock will take us beyond their sensors and we will head to the Katherine Hub, virtually invisible. From there I go to New

Prague. You are welcome to come with me. I am not forcing you into anything."

If Sirn is dead, then I'm free. Sirn had loomed so large for so long, she felt dizzy at the idea of being free of him.

"If Sirn is dead, then I could return to my homeworld. But if he is alive, I can't go to Coloun. They would alert him to my presence."

"Even if Sirn is dead I do not think you should go back to Coloun. I do not think you are ready for such a journey by yourself, little queen."

"What do you mean?"

"I mean you would be in rough, lawless places, with people you can't trust. Since Sirn's invasion, the treaties and contracts that kept the hubs and common lanes orderly and safe are gone. Far different than an Emperor's luxurious palace."

He thought she was useless and weak. That knowledge made her feel awful. Blood rushed up into her face. "I think I would manage. And how do you know, anyway? You've been a cyborg for years. And quit calling me little queen. I have a name."

"All right. Sabralia." He grinned in a cocky way. Then his expression got more serious. "Even longer than three years ago the rule of law was ripped away from this system. It became each world for themselves, which made the way even easier for Sirn's Forces. I think you would be better off staying in New Prague."

Sabralia didn't reply to that. Kaistril seemed very certain of what she should do, while she was not certain at all.

"How long will it take to reach New Prague?"

"It will take us six weeks to reach Katherine Hub. From there we will have to contact my family, so they can bring a jump ship to us. This vehicle has no jump capabilities. We would never get to New Prague in it. We could take commercial jump passage, but I would rather wait for my family."

"Right," she said, feeling a little faint. "Your family has access to jump ships?"

"Yes. But even if they didn't, we could find a public transport to the Hub nearest New Prague. Public transports are often the target of pirates and raiders, so they are not my first choice for travel."

She finished eating. Kaistril showed her how to use the hygenie to clean everything, and they cleaned the dishes together. When everything was cleaned up she turned to go sit on one of the upholstered chairs, not knowing what to do next. Kaistril followed her and stood so close she could feel the heat of his legs against her knees.

"Come, Sabralia. We need to go to bed."

"What?" Her heart gave a hard thud and she jumped up, shaking with tension.

He grinned. "Not that. Not yet, anyway. I need sleep so I can take care of the tracer tomorrow. It is a complex issue. As a cyborg I did not feel fatigue, but now I do as a man. I will leave you to the stateroom, and sleep at the command center. The chairs convert for comfort." He turned and left her alone.

Sabralia went back to the luxurious stateroom. She wasn't really ready to sleep and she was pleased to find a collection of readers. Sliding one into her arm com, she crawled under the covers and tried to relax. It was so odd to be sleeping by herself. She found it very hard to relax. Part of her listened beyond the telling of the story for movement, for Qy�-Kaistril to come to the stateroom. She finally got up to peek at him. He was sound asleep in a reclining com chair. She returned to her book, a romance about an Etherian poet and a Star Woman Priestess. She ended up staying awake far past the time she could have slept to read the story to its satisfying end. Maybe her own life would have a love like that, someday. Maybe her future wasn't a bleak one, under Sirn's shadow.

Sabralia woke and checked her com. She'd slept several hours after finally falling asleep. She used the bath and braided her hair before entering the main room. Kaistril was up, sitting in the ship's control seat. His fingers fairly flew over the ship's key panel and data flipped across the viewer.

Sabralia helped herself to a cup of Kaf and a fruit cup. Once she finally fell asleep, she'd slept hard and she felt only half awake now. Kaistril looked far too robust and energetic.

"What are you doing up? You stayed up very late."

"I think it is the strange room. It was hard to sleep." She didn't want to mention that she was used to sleeping in the arms of her cyborg, skin to skin.

Kaistril turned toward her. "I should have looked through Alfyt's belongings earlier." He held up a cube of info films. Alfyt's bags were open on the floor next to the control panel.

"What's in them?" Curious, she slid into the co-command chair and looked through the bags. Jewels were knotted and tangled together in the bag. Sabralia picked up a strand of iridescent beads and started to untangle the mess. A fortune. And more info film. The other, smaller bag held mundane clothing and toiletries.

"Tons of data, along with priceless jewels from the harem." Kaistril slid one wafer into a data slot on the ship's com. "I don't think it is Alfyt's personal library. I think he was being very, very disloyal to his Emperor. It's all encrypted. This could be very good, or very bad."

"What do you mean?"

"He was probably heading toward a Puregen world, where he could sell the information."

"You think it might be Sirn's? Military information?"

"Yes. And if anyone knows he had it, they might try hard to find it." Kaistril tapped orders on his com. Then he ejected the films from the ship's com and slipped them one by one into a small opening on his thigh implant.

"The ship may not be able to read the encryption on some of these. They'll be recorded in my appliance. Always good to have a back up. And maybe my appliances have a key for decryption."

When the films were put away in their little cubes, Kaistril asked, "You ready to get to work?"

Sabralia looked at him blankly. She hadn't worked on anything since her school years. "What should I do?"

"I'm going to show you what to do while I'm fixing the tracer." He tapped keys on the command panel and soon a view of the hull showed. "See this red dot? This toggle switch moves it around." He demonstrated the device.

"I'm going to be out there, so your job is to keep this dot trained on me. It is set to track me. If I send a distress signal"—he pressed a button and a loud whistle filled the ship—"or if you see something happen, like my cord comes loose, or a piece of equipment cracks me in the head, or if I am unresponsive, you press this red button. There's a smart line that will grab me before I float out. My other tethers will detach and I will be drawn into the lower level hold. It's a failsafe to keep me from drifting out into space."

"You have to go out in the vacuum?" The thought horrified her. Space work was so dangerous, hardly anyone did it. They used sucker ships that attached to the area of the hull needing work, for the safety of the technicians. Space suits were only used in emergencies.

"Well, yes. The tracer is under the hull. They don't make them easy to get rid of. Now follow me down to the hold so I can show you how to open the hatches. I have Life support running while we are working on this."

She followed him down to the lower level.

The hold level had a low ceiling, so Kaistril had to duck his head through all the hatches. It was one long hallway, with small cramped workstations along the sides, some with shallow com stations and utilitarian stools. Nothing luxurious about the crew quarters. One area held four narrow bunks. She followed him through a small door outlined in red.

"This is the med station. Emergency sleep tubes are in here. I'm going to show you that, too. If anything happens to me, you'll be stranded. You'll have to get into a tube. If I'm alive, but gravely injured, you'll want to get me into one, too."

"O-Of course." Horror gripped her at the thought.

"I've set a beacon on these that is an emergency frequency for the New Prague military. It has a special signature that identifies me. I believe we would be picked up in less than a year. These particular tubes only have energy for two years, so I made the beacon urgent."

Sabralia couldn't help the involuntary shiver. "After that, they are coffins! It's dangerous—this ship, the tracer. This is all very dangerous."

She'd known safety as a girl, before Sirn. And even as a wife in the harem, she had felt safe. The war was fought far away, or so she'd thought.

Kaistril turned and looked at her. "Here, do you need to sit down? Your face is a little white."

She sat on a small examination chair. "I'm sorry. You probably think I'm very weak. Useless. You are very brave about all this."

"No! That's not what I think at all. It's different for me." He paused for a moment, then knelt down in front of her and took her hand. "I've been on small spacecrafts half my life. In the military, in battles. I've been in a sleep tube, for training. Drills were routine, part of ship life. I've been trained in hull repair, in a vacuum, too." He wiped a tear from the corner of her eye. "Take a few deep breaths, Sabra. I truly believe we will be fine."

She breathed and tried to calm herself. "You learned this in the military?"

"I went into a military academy at age twelve, as did all my brothers. My parents wanted us prepared for the life we would have to live on New Prague, with Sirn's Forces so near. So none of this is new to me, like it is to you. Now come look at these tubes so you'll know what to do."

The tube access panels were on the floor. Automated audio explained how to undress and pull on the cover and face mask that would mold to the body. It really wasn't complicated. She climbed inside and performed the drill so she could do it if necessary.

"Sabra, if something does happen to me, and you have to put me in a tube, don't wait to get in one yourself. Not even a moment. Don't go get anything, just get into the tube and launch."

"All right."

"Here's a float." He indicated a padded board attached to the wall. "You just press these pads, then pull it by hand, easy. You pull me into the hold, pressurize it, float me to the tubes, get me out of my suit, and stuff me in a tube. Don't try to do anything medical. I'll be all right in the tube until we're found. Then get into one yourself and tell the com to launch us."

"And later we'll be rescued by New Prague forces?" She wanted the reassurance.

"Yes, we'll be rescued."

Kaistril showed her how to pressurize the small hold he would enter and exit from, and how to close everything up properly. He had her repeat the lesson, then showed her a key on the panel that would walk her through if she forgot.

"I won't forget," Sabralia said, somewhat indignantly.

"I know. But if something bad happened, you might forget for a moment."

"You think something bad might happen?" Her voice was high-pitched.

"No. But it is best to know what to do in a worst case scenario."

As nice as the chameleon hull was to use, it was hell getting through the circuitry. The only thing keeping Kaistril from sweating hard was the sophisticated temperature system of his space suit. He appreciated well-made equipment, and the small cruiser had the best of the best for a ship of its size.

But even with this great equipment, the removal of the tracer was taking far too long. He'd have to recalculate fuel, since getting through this hull was so time consuming and ate up an amazing amount of energy.

His sensors hadn't alerted him even once to space debris, which was good. He didn't need that kind of distraction.

"Are you all right?" Sabralia checked on him every few minutes, even though she could see him moving, and knew he was definitely not unconscious. She still sounded nervous.

He grinned. "Yes, I'm well. This is just taking much longer than I thought."

"Do you think you should quit?"

"Can't quit. This is vital." They needed to be lost to Sirn's equipment.

There was a pause. "I'll check on you in five."

Sabralia was a good woman. The kind who should settle down on some calm world far from Sirn and raise a family. Bake sweet buns for her children.

Not his type at all. The women he chose were hard military women, athletic, ready for robust sex, and then to go off to their next command duty. No ties, just good sex, jokes, stimulating conversation, a few drinks in a cantina. They would hook up while on leave, consume food, intoxicants, and each other, then return to the responsibilities of their command after a relaxing, pleasant interlude.

A vision of Sabralia, naked in her bath at the palace, came to him. Big, round, pink-tipped breasts, silky skin, those dimples above the round globes of ass he'd like to squeeze...He wanted her. The years spent as her cyborg were part of him now, and when he looked back on that time it was with a man's passion. All those months in the bath teased him, ratcheting up his desire. He had the memories of the times she had asked for his touch...of kissing, cupping those heavy breasts while washing her.

What he needed was a good pounding fuck, but he wouldn't get that here. More than likely he would say or do something crude and terrify her. She was already half afraid of him, and he couldn't blame her since she so narrowly avoided being raped by Sirn's Best. Plus, she'd been married to Sirn, who was known to be a real pig.

He wondered when she'd notice his frequent hard-ons. And if they did fall into bed together...it would feel great, but she was not the type who would move on to her next lover with no regrets. She might get hurt, thinking he was the man who would give her those babies.

He sighed. They would be alone on the small ship for a long time. A healthy man and a woman alone...things could happen. But would it be a good idea to have sex with her?

Not that he would have the will power to resist if the opportunity came.

And were they fertile? Hell, he should try and find that out.

The sooner they got to New Prague and he deposited her into safe hands, the better. His mother would know what to do with her. Sabralia deserved a chance at having a good life.

Finally, he reached the tracer and severed it from the power supply. Yes!

Sabralia pressurized the loading dock and opened the hatch when it was ready. "Are you all right? You were out there seven hours." Her dark blue eyes were huge. He grinned. It was kind of nice to have someone worry about him.

"I'm fine. Tired. Help me out of this, all right?" In the light grav of the ship, the suit had a crushing weight.

She helped him out of the gear, and helped him stash it in its diagnostic chamber. No flashing lights, the suit was undamaged.

"I cooked a meal."

He followed her up the stairs. Sabralia wasn't wearing Alfyt's jacket and her round bottom was only a hand's breath from his face. He wanted to sink his teeth into a round globe, run a finger down that sweet crack...

"Food sounds good." His voice sounded funny, so he cleared his throat.

She turned around, eyes round with concern. "Are you all right? You sound like you're getting sick."

Her breasts, covered in the thin knit, were right in his face, nipples clearly outlined. He knew he was staring and it was crude, but he couldn't stop. It was all he could do to keep his hands from cupping those lush breasts.

"I don't get sick," he croaked out. "Puregen immune system."

"Oh. You probably need something to drink." She turned and went onto the main deck.

He didn't tell her the suit had a hydration and glucose system. Kaistril took a steadying breath and followed her. He sat down quickly at the table so she wouldn't see his erection.

This was going to be one long journey.

Chapter Five

"SO WE HAVE A HUNDRED and twenty days of this? Nothing?" Sabralia said the morning of their fourth day in transit. Kaistril checked ship's systems while Sabralia followed him around, bored.

He glanced at her, amused. "You have traveled in space before."

She shrugged. "I was on a sleep transport."

He raised his eyebrows. "And how did that work out?"

She wrinkled her nose. "I was sick for a week when I woke up. That was on Sirn's jump ship that I met at Katherine Hub. And then I got to have my wedding night. But at least by then I was over the nausea."

"Hardly anyone uses those sleep transports anymore. They must be almost a century old."

"Coloun isn't a tech world. Mostly we shipped grains and farm produce."

"So Sirn made a treaty with your world for produce?"

"Yes. All of our crops, minus what we needed, went to his supply chain. I think there was more to it, though."

Kaistril raised an eyebrow.

"I think he planned to bring farmers from Coloun to his Jewel. It has a climate that would work well for agriculture. There are even a few farms on the outskirts of the Palace complex. I think having me there as a token queen would make the farmers come more willingly."

Kaistril nodded. "It is easier to have a workforce that is willing to work. And a military force requires huge amounts of food." He walked to a display panel and tapped on his com. Sabralia followed him like a puppy.

"What are you doing now?"

He sighed, then grinned at her. "Would you like me to teach you how to do a systems check?"

"Really? You think I could learn that?" Her eyes widened and she fairly glowed.

He couldn't help smiling at her. "Without a doubt."

Sabra was delighted to learn the system's checks. Some involved mathematics that she had no background in, but Kaistril patiently taught her on printouts from the com. She spent several days learning the formulas, and how to double check and triple check the input on the com.

"You always triple check. One mistake could leave a ship off-mark, stranded. This ship gets lost, and we're in the tubes when the fuel burns up."

Kaistril was thorough and exacting. She worked hard. A few days later, she did a complete systems check by herself, correctly.

"Now I want to learn how to pilot!"

Kaistril laughed. "Why not? We'll start tomorrow."

Flying actually came easier to her than system's checks. The checks involved formulas and calculations, flying involved reflexes and vision.

Since they were in deep space with nothing around them, Kaistril set probes out, which she maneuvered through. It was fun, like a game, and there was no danger she'd crash into anything.

She learned how to use the focal device, which told her the amounts of clearance she had, fuel burn ratios, all types of things.

"How come you don't use the focal?" she asked Kaistril.

"My com." He tapped the silver device on his thigh. "It is connected to the ship's system, and tells me all that info."

"Do you see it? Like I do—burn ratios in red, clearance distance in blue?"

He shook his head. "No. I would if I still had the temple appliance. Now it is more like a knowing, a thought."

"Why did you take that off? Not that I mind."

He gave her an arch look. "I did it for you, baby. To dazzle you with my manly good looks."

She giggled. "No, really."

He shrugged. "I figured it might have a kill function. Why take the chance?"

"Oh." What if he'd died? She swallowed hard. "Do you think it is safe to keep those?" She waved her hand, indicating his arm and thigh appliances.

"I think so. They are different than the temple piece. These are some type of new technology, very sophisticated. I want to show them to my father."

"Your father?"

"He's a scientist, very brilliant."

He couldn't help it, he yawned. Sleeping near the lights of the console wasn't ideal. Plus thoughts of Sara often kept him awake. Sabra noticed his yawn."I didn't sleep well." He waved a hand at the console. "The lights."

"We could take turns with the stateroom." Sabralia bit her lower lip. She wanted more than to share the stateroom. Being constant companions with him every day, she wanted his touch. Now that she was no longer afraid of him, she craved his time and attention, and alone in her bed at night, she relived the bathing pool, except instead of the cyborg, Qy, she was bathed by Kaistril, the warrior.

Did she dare? They were only fourteen days from Katherine Hub, and soon they would go their separate ways. She would follow him to New Prague because she really had nowhere else to go. If Sirn was alive, her homeworld wouldn't be a safe place for her.

Kaistril would go back to his Tier. She suspected he was a high-ranking officer, perhaps a commander in the military. He would join his Tier and fight to keep his world free.

He wanted her, she knew. Sometimes they brushed against each other at the control com, and a few times she saw the hard ridge of his erection under the spacer knits. Sometimes a brief touch would empty both their minds of thought and they would just stare at each other for a moment, breathing in anticipation...but neither of them made a move.

"Sleep with me in the stateroom, Kaistril." Her voice was soft.

Kaistril's shoulders tightened and his body froze. Then he whirled up and out of the com chair so fast she felt dizzy. He came very close, so close she had to look up, so close she could feel the heat of his body and it made her skin tingle in awareness.

"Sooner than we know, we will be in New Prague. We may never see each other again. I will return to my warriors and fight for our freedom, while you will settle in some safe place, where you will no doubt marry and produce many pretty babies."

His hand trailed up her neck and traced the crevice of her lips. "Once I rejoin my Tier, I will not have time to be with a woman for many long days...and they won't be sweet and soft, like you."

Years of wanting her cyborg to be a man, not a cyborg, made her weak. He was a man—more aggressive than she'd ever imagined, but still a man. Real. Sabralia sagged against him, pressing her breasts against his hard chest.

"I should leave you alone," he whispered close to her lips. She slid her hands up his hard chest, then around his neck.

"I may still be married to Sirn," she whispered.

"You will never go back to that marriage. I will see it is ended in accordance with New Prague law. But...are you sure?"

She pulled his head down and pressed her lips to his, trembling with the knowledge that she was going to be so intimate with Kaistril, that it would be real, not a lonely woman's dream.

Kaistril's kiss was nothing like Qy's kisses. This was an invasion, hard, insistent, deep. Electrical. Steel strong arms captured her tight, one hand cupped her head. His tongue was demanding, but still a velvet caress. So different from the kiss of a cyborg. So much better. She met his tongue with her own, shivering with delight and shock.

Kaistril picked her up with an easy swing and took her to the bedroom, where he let her body slide slowly to the floor in front of the bed. He fell with her to the soft bed, drawing her tight to his side, the length of his body molded against hers. His hand gently stroked her hair and face, then slid around her neck, massaging gently, just the way she liked. One large hand cupped her breast, and she drew in a breath at the tingling pleasure.

"I remember my mistress who slept naked in my arms, the round naked flesh glistening as I bathed her, the long hours of deep kisses." He leaned back. "As a cyborg, I did not know what the cleansing spray was all about, here." He drew a finger between her legs, right over her clit, and she jumped.

"But now I am a man again. I know. Those memories will not be my torment." His face came very close and he gripped her head with two hands. "We will sate each other, put those longings to rest..." His voice was a husky whisper against her lips. The kiss deepened, and he slid onto her so they lay full length together.

He pulled away from her lips and his hot breath brushed her neck. "And you will for once know what it is like to be with a man, not a selfish Emperor or an ignorant cyborg. I will pleasure you, and you will not have to tell me what to do, only if you like it." Kaistril's low, raspy voice went straight to her core, both electrifying and melting her.

He maneuvered her shirt off and leaned over, aggressive, overwhelming, and his hungry mouth devoured a nipple. "You do not have to school me in what to do. I probably know more what needs to be done in this situation than you do, little queen."

His wet tongue flicked and rubbed her nipple. She moaned softly, shocked at the pleasure. He did it again, large, hard hands cupping her while his lips and tongue feasted on her nipples.

"Your breasts are so lovely. I have dreamed of tasting them as a man."

He pulled his mouth away, grabbed one of her hands, and moved it to his crotch, pressing it to his rock hard erection under the thin knits. "This is another thing you don't need to command into being."

"Q-Qy—" She gasped.

"—Kaistril," he growled, crushing his lips against hers. The kiss ran like lightning through her veins, and she kissed him back, winding her hands in his felt-like locks. He raised his head and she dragged in a breath. His eyes shimmered with pleasure and lust, his lips curved into a slight smile. He was more beautiful than in any of her imaginings.

"I'm weak and useless. Not a warrior woman like you enjoy." Sabralia voiced her confusion. And then she felt awful, so sad. Tears welled into her eyes. "I was never trained to do anything. I was married to Sirn before my schooling was done."

Her lack of knowledge or skills for life outside the harem was a heavy weight on her mind.

"Ahh, sweet one. You are soft and gentle. The military women of my world like to fight and tussle before they bed a man, but you are not like that. There is no harm in you, and I would never need to sleep with my weapon near, with you in my bed. And that pleases me."

His finger caressed her lips, and his mouth gently kissed away her tears. She couldn't look away from his eyes that looked so deep into her own. She felt open and vulnerable. He knew her so well, but she didn't know him at all.

"Do you know that we warriors fight to protect women like you? Women who raise the children, oversee the communities and homesteads, make our lives warm and joyful, who are kind even to a brain-dead cyborg." Sabralia could barely breathe. Qy—Kaistril—wanted to make love to her. He thought she was a worthy person, despite her lack of skills. Like she'd dreamed about for so long.

"Kiss me like you did when I was a cyborg," he entreated, brushing his lips against hers, and at that moment she realized that there was vulnerability under his warrior's exterior. She tangled her hands into his hair and pulled him close until she could trace his full lips with her tongue. He quickly opened his mouth and groaned deep in his throat when she sucked his tongue, as he thrust his in and out, her mind spinning. He was her anchor, she gripped his shoulders tight.

"This reminds me of something." Kaistril's eyes twinkled at her. He pulled at her leggings, then stood and ripped off his clothes.

She swallowed. She'd seen him naked before, many times. His body was perfect—defined abs and thigh muscles, broad shoulders, narrow hips. She'd never seen him erect. But now his cock seemed to strain toward her, an aggressive red, the head plump and round, moist at the slit.

"These need to come off." Kaistril pulled off her boots and leggings.

Exposed in her bareness, Sabralia slid a hand to cover herself. Qy the cyborg never really noticed if she was naked or clothed, but Kaistril's gaze was intense.

"How long was I your lady's maid?" His voice was husky.

"Two years, almost three." Her voice was breathy.

"Three years. I must have seen you naked a hundred times."

"Daily. You bathed me daily." Her boots and leggings fell to the floor.

"Yes, hundreds of times." His voice had a raspy quality to it that made a shiver run through her. With quick, strong hands, he pulled her legs up and out exposing her. Instinctively, her hands moved to cover her most intimate parts, but his hands held hers away.

"Ah, ah now. This is something the cyborg never got to see. I plan to look my fill." He knelt down before her and she swallowed, barely able to breathe.

Embarrassment made her tighten her legs, ready to slam them back together.

Kaistril looked up at her and grinned broadly. He smoothed hot, strong hands along her thighs, up to her bottom, where he massaged her, deeply. "Now, don't be shy. You must know I find you lovely."

His eyes focused on her exposed flesh. "Glistening petals. You are wet for me." One long finger made a line through her curls, over her clit, and then pressed deep inside. He withdrew his finger and tugged gently on her small labia. "I think I should call you Petal."

He leaned closer and breathed deep of her essence. "The flower is sweet. I wonder how you taste."

She whimpered, feeling more moisture gliding, then his tongue did a long, slow lick from her wet pool, up to her clit. His finger spread her plump lips, and his lips gently nibbled the small, delicate inner petals.

Nothing had ever felt so good. Sabralia twined her finger into his locks, to keep him close. Her legs trembled with the sweetness of his touch.

His mouth latched onto her clit, and suctioned. She flew apart, with a gasping cry she didn't recognize as her own, shattering into sparkling pleasure.

Kaistril immediately flowed up her body, one heavy thigh pinning her to the bed, hands gliding everywhere, cupping her breasts. His breath was hot and fast as he nuzzled her neck."I'm not much like Qy, am I?"

"No."

"Do you miss him?"

"He...I was comfortable with you. Him."

"But you never rode him, you never had him make you come, except with the bathing sprayer."

"No."

"I think I know why." He breathed between kisses that were slowly moving toward her breasts.

"Why?" she asked. She couldn't think why. Her pussy still throbbed with pleasure, her breasts strained for his touch.

"I think you didn't want to ride a passive cock. Not a bot you had to school in every move. I think you wanted a warrior between your thighs." His mouth latched onto a nipple in a fevered caress that soon had her moaning. His leg was between her, and she wrapped both hers around his hips as he continued to lick and rub her nipples. One hand pushed between her legs. One finger found her clit. His touch was firm, but so slow. She wiggled against him impatiently, but still he caressed her slow, pausing at her pussy for a moment.

"Kaistril," she moaned as he left her clit again, finger pressing deep.

"Is this what you want, little queen?" His voice was ragged. Then he was on top of her, and his cock pressed into her so quickly she lost her breath. She was stretched to accommodate his girth, but the stretching was delicious, not painful, filling her in a way that was so right and necessary she wondered how she'd lived without it.

He pulled out in such a way that his wet cock slid over her clit, then plunged back in, almost too rough, pushing her higher, then back up against her clit. The intensity of pleasure nearly took her breath away, and she gasped for air.

He surged deep, hard, over and over until she came in a glorious rush, crying out and clutching him tight with her legs and her pussy. With a hoarse cry, he rammed into her, and she felt the wash of his come fill her.

"Are you all right?" Kaistril asked after, his tone husky. "I got a little wild there toward the end." His eyes searched her face.

"It was wonderful. I didn't know it could be like that," she whispered, feeling suddenly shy. She buried her face against the curve of his neck, breathing deep of his masculine scent and gliding a hand through his felt locks, which still somehow felt silky.

"Are you tired?"

She giggled. "No. I slept fine."

Kaistril took a deep breath, his chest pressing tight to her breasts. He breathed out audibly. "Good. Because I would really like to do that again."

Sabralia ran her lips over his shoulder, reveling in his smooth, muscled form.

"Of course we can do that again. I loved it."

Kaistril rolled her onto her back and wedged his knees between her legs. His thick cock slid slowly between her swollen slick lips. "I mean, do it again right now."

A rush of heat swept through her and she clasped her legs around his slim hips. Sabralia met his eyes, which were dark, intense.

"I didn't know you could so soon." She wiggled her hips, caressing the round head of his cock with her movements.

Kaistril pushed inside, just a little way. "You know you've uncaged the beast, don't you?" he groaned.

Sabralia clutched him tight to her with legs and arms, and he slid deeper into her. "Maybe I'll tame him," she whispered, pulling his mouth down to hers.

Chapter Six

SABRALIA AWOKE ALONE in bed one night a weeks later. Only a few hours of their sleep cycle had passed, so she was a little surprised she was alone. They had reverted to the way they had slept together as mistress and cyborg, spooned naked together.

All the lights were powered down. She entered the main room. Kaistril was at the com.

"Couldn't you sleep?"

His lips curved in welcome, but he shrugged. "The encryption is finally removed. I opened my case file."

"Oh." He seemed so...somber. "Is there something wrong?"

He reached for her and pulled her onto his lap. Sabralia stared at him, alarmed. Normally such a move was a prelude to sex, but he wasn't hard.

"What?"

He looked away. "There's a failsafe."

She was silent for a moment. "On the ship?"

"No. In me." He tapped his temple where the appliance once sat.

Understanding dawned, followed by clutching horror.

"Will it kill you?" Nausea welled up her throat.

"I don't think so. I got the temple device off pretty early on. In the event of missing maintenance procedures, the temple device sends in nanos that are supposed to shut the cyborg down, but not damage it."

"Shut you down? Like kill you?"

"I don't believe so. They don't like to destroy something they've put so much research and resources into. I was an experiment. All the cyborgs in the harem were experiments. Sooner or later Sirn would have moved me to military duties. They just want to shut the cyborg down until they can collect it and recondition it, if it begins to remember."

"Is someone coming to collect you?" she asked, horrified.

"None of our sensors indicate anyone is following us. But eventually someone will notice this ship is gone. A ship like this is worth the gross national product of some planets."

"When do you think the failsafe will start?"

"I think it already has. I am tired, but I can't sleep. Puregens recover quickly, so I am rarely tired. None of my activities should tire me."

"What about the weight bearing exercises? Are you doing many of those?"

"Just the normal sequence. Nothing that would make me tired."

"What can I do?"

"We're going to dock at Katherine Hub in just a few days. I don't know how responsive I will be by then, but we can get a prerecorded message zipped to New Prague. It'll cost, but it is a common service on the hubs." He tapped the com and showed her.

"I have it all set. My brothers will come for you."

"Us."

He nodded and gave her a crooked smile. Her heart raced in fear. This was serious.

"You'll need to find secure housing and a reputable buyer for the jewels to pay for lodging. The ship is worth a great deal, but it will be recognized if we try to sell it. We need to just abandon it so we can't be traced to it at the Hub. Hopefully my brothers can retrieve it when they get us."

"I think will have more physical maladies than mental ones. The purpose of the nanos is to shut me down so I can be retrieved. I think they will make me unconscious but keep me alive."

Sabralia pulled his face close to hers. "I'll get you to New Prague. We'll get you help."

"It should be all right, after awhile. The nanos will not have a power supply. I'm removing my other appliances."

She uncurled from his lap in shock. "I thought they were fitted too deep and removing could knick your arteries. Isn't that very dangerous?"

"We're not going to do it unless it is absolutely necessary. Once we get to Katherine Hub, we'll hire a medic. But we should go over the procedure tomorrow, after you've slept. Just in case. If there is trouble, there are medics on the Hub."

Kaistril insisted she go back to bed.

"I can't possibly sleep now, Kaistril."

He captured her face in one large hand, and his mouth, open and hot, came down over hers. He crushed her against his chest, firm hands sliding down her back to her bottom. Sweeping her up into his arms, he carried her back to the bed. "Maybe we can help each other sleep."

The next day was busy, as she learned about Katherine Hub's docking procedures and practices. Sabralia was so thankful she'd spent the weeks in transit learning how to do systems checks and pilot.

Kaistril...she could see a difference. He didn't sleep, but often spent long moments just sitting and staring. His speech became slower. Kaistril's movements were jerky and hard to control. Sabralia cried, quietly, in the bath, especially when she remembered how he'd run with her in his arms, to safety. She wanted to just take him to the big bed and cuddle with him, but there was too much to do.

"Sabra, come put some data in for me, all right?"

He was sitting at the com. She did what he asked.

"Look." Kaistril pointed out a screen with two bright spots. "We're being followed."

"Will they catch up with us?"

"I don't think so. Sirn does—did—have craft that could jump and catch us, but no commander would send something like that after us. They probably want the ship more than they want us. I doubt they know about the film." He stretched.

"I'm functioning better than I thought I would. We can wait until we get to the Hub to remove the appliances." His speech was labored, and he sat at the controls, looking tired and drawn. "It wouldn't be a great idea to go into the sleep tubes. They'd find us right away. Unless there is a full power failure, we stay on course."

"How did they find us?"

"I guess they figured we were on our way to Katherine Hub. And they may not have sensed us yet, because of the chameleon hull. I dumped sensors along the way so I would know if anyone was traveling toward the hub."

Sabralia checked the monitors. "We'll be at the Hub in sixty-six hours."

"Hopefully I'll be alert."

Kaistril was awake but slow to respond the rest of the day.

"Make cloak...men see you."

Her choice of clothing was her transparent dress or the spacer knits with Alfyt's jacket, both very revealing.

"Right. I should make a cover up."

There was a tailoring device. She used it to turn some of the bedding into a loose gown and cloak.

"Are you coming to bed?" she asked as their sleep cycle approached.

Kaistril was at the com, running some type of report.

"You go ahead. I'll be there in a little while."

Sabralia fell asleep waiting for him. She awoke some hours later, still alone in the bed. She went out to see what Kaistril was doing.

He was at the com, but slumped to one side. He was blinking rapidly.

Something is wrong!

"Kaistril. Kaistril are you all right?" He did not respond.

Oh no, oh no. She adjusted his chair so he was lying down. He felt hot. She ran to the lavatory for a wet cloth. She bathed his face.

His temperature was high, he was burning up. "Kaistril, we should get you into the shower. Can you walk?"

He did not respond. She tried to pull him up, but could not get him out of the chair.

The appliances had to come off. They couldn't wait two days—he could be dead in two days.

She tapped on the com until she found the file Kaistril had saved, on removing the appliances. Her fingers shook as she tapped the controls. She started to rush through the file, then stopped and took a deep breath.

Kaistril needed her to know how to do this procedure to survive. She studied it for close to an hour, then assembled her supplies. The ship's medic kit was well stocked.

"Kaistril, I'm going to give you a neurosed, so I can take the appliances off. Can you swallow?"

He did not respond.

She tried giving him a sip of water. It dribbled out.

The medkit contained a synthesizer. She put the neurosed in that and sprayed it up his nose. Then she undressed him, which was a heavy job.

Next, the cleaning. She scrubbed him until his skin was bright pink.

There were five vials of wound sealant. She would use two on his arm and three on his leg. She hoped that would be enough. If he bled heavily, she didn't have the equipment or skill to save his life.

Sabralia took a vial to his leg. It was made to harvest a small amount of flesh, to blend with the medical nano technology to seal the wound. It left a small bloody wound.

Sabralia covered it with a patch and then had to sit down. There was going to be blood. Maybe a lot of it. Was she really going to go through with it?

She looked at Kaistril. His face was pale and beaded with sweat, slack in unconsciousness. All his vitality had been stripped away, leaving him vulnerable and even weaker than she was.

Yes. She would remove the appliances.

She finished the vials, then set the pressure point devices, to slow the blood flow on his arm. With that, she took the scalpel, pried his arm com up with her fingers, and slit into his arm so the device could be pulled free.

There was blood. She pulled the appliance off as quickly as she could, then applied pressure to the wound for a moment.

She had to get the nanoseal as close to the artery wound as possible. Sabralia set the device for higher pressure, then swabbed the area until she could find the torn artery. She squeezed two vials into it, then padded it heavily. After the prescribed time, she loosened the pressure point device, while keeping pressure on the arm with her hands. Blood seeped through the pad. She added another and pressed hard again.

There was no time to panic, but her heart was racing.

Her arms, shoulder, and neck ached from pressing down on his arm. Finally, she was able to raise her hands without seeing blood color the pad.

She wrapped his arm tightly and checked his fingers. They looked all right to her, a little pale...but not blue.

She slumped into the console chair. The thigh would be harder.

It was finally over. Kaistril had lost more blood than she had hoped, but she was able to add to his fluid levels, and the com said his readings were in acceptable limits. Hopefully his Puregen heritage helped him heal really fast. She'd heard that was so.

Sabralia taped his arm and legs to the chair to keep them still as he woke. The nanoseals would be set in three hours, and she had no more. She tucked a soft body warmer around him.

She was splattered with blood, and the consul area was a mess. Slowly, Sabralia cleaned up the cloths and pads, and disposed of the empty vials. Her arms and legs felt like lead, and her head pounded. She stumbled to the shower and cleaned off quickly. Her hands and legs were shaking with shock.

After changing into new garments, she remembered that a systems check needed to be done. She grabbed a cup of Kaf, which she drank as quickly as possible, then ate a quick meal that sat like lead in her stomach.

The systems check took longer than usual, but she did it right, like Kaistril had taught her, and triple checked. The memory of Kaistril grinning and joking, yet expecting her to be so exact in doing a systems check, came to her. Star Goddess above, would he ever be that way again?

Sabralia checked Kaistril every few minutes, thankful he remained stable. Finally, she grabbed another warmer, set a timer to wake her every half hour, and collapsed into the consul chair next to him, and fell asleep.

An alarm woke her. She leaped to Kaistril, heart thundering in panic.

The com showed all his systems were fine.

She looked around in confusion.

"Clean the appliances." Kaistril's voice was rough. He spoke without opening his eyes. "Nano...won't transmit now...my body the energy source."

"Kaistril! Are you all right? How do you feel?" "Right."

He was awake. Tears of joy flowed as she checked him. He finally opened his eyes and looked at the console."After us. Increase speed.

Check systems. We should be able to burst for awhile. They know we're headed for the Hub, but we can hide there. Get off ship."

"I can do that. We've made it this far." She held his cold hand tight.

"You did good," Kaistril whispered, then fell back asleep.

Sabralia rushed to shoot the appliances into the hygenie, then set speed and did a systems check. She still felt exhausted, but Kaistril's com reports were still good.

Much later, Kaistril awoke again. He groaned. Sabralia leaped out of her chair to his side.

"What's wrong? Are you bleeding?" She checked his wounds. They looked sealed, with no blood. Bleeding was the greatest danger. "No. Feel fine. Can't move much."

She removed the tape from his arm and legs. He still didn't move. "You can't move?"

Had she paralyzed him?

"Sure I can move. Just don't want to. Feel weak." He waved an arm then dropped it back to the recliner.

"Oh. Well, that is one of the normal side-effects of the removal."

"Yes. Thinking and speaking are...effort." Sabralia smiled in relief. "It is working! When I decided to take them out you were unresponsive, but you weren't really asleep, either. Your eyes were blinking so fast. Soon you will be able to walk and no appliances will shut you down." She ran kisses over his face.

When she stood up he held up his arm with the fluid pouch attached to it. "I think you can take this out. I can eat and drink now."

Sabralia got the medkit to take off the fluid pouch, and Kaistril drank a meal replacement, then went back to sleep. She stroked his hair for awhile. He was going to be all right.

Kaistril slept for most of the next day, though he did move around a little, to the hygiene chamber and the comfortable bed, with her help. He was lucid for small amounts of time.

"Sabralia," he whispered during one of his brief moments of full consciousness. "Sorry I can't help."

"That is all right. I just want you to get better."

He fell asleep, lips curved into a slight smile.

Kaistril slept while she got into the queue to dock at Katherine Hub, which was easier than moving between the probes Kaistril had made her practice on. The com no longer showed anyone following them, but they would queue up also, several hours behind them.

Six hours before docking, Kaistril awoke. "Sabra, need help with the com." She helped him to the com, then gave him a meal replacement drink while he tapped slowly, with just one hand. "I'll sleep here. Link ups...for my family com..."

His eyes fluttered shut and she eased him back into the seat, leaned it back, and strapped him down for docking.

"First," he said, though his eyes were closed. "Send message first thing at docking." Once they were docked they could use Katherine Hub's communication service, which was necessary because the small ship need a boost to get a message to New Prague.

It did make sense. Send the message first, before they left the ship. She looked at the com routes and saw he had geared all replies to her arm com. He must have written this some time ago and saved it. Geared to her personal com, they could receive the message anywhere on the Hub.

Sabralia made sure her arm com was powered up. There would be no natural sunlight on the Hub, but the com had a small device that could draw power from most ordinary power grids. Then she changed into the concealing gown and packed Alfryt's bags with the jewels and info cubes they were taking with them. She was ready.

Katherine Hub was an enormous space-built spiral of docking bays, surrounding a central globe complex from which the many spiral arms sprang. There was a government of sorts, run by the trade guilds, but they mainly dealt with tariffs and commodity inspections. The complex was known for its wild lawlessness, danger and ruthless trade guild mercs who dealt with any trouble without a trial or any type of process of law. Hundreds of people lived on the Hub, working on the space docks, markets and eateries.

The docking procedure was similar to simulated ones she'd done over and over in the past days. She docked with no trouble at all.

"Kaistril. Wake up! I did it. We're docked!"

Her excitement must have reached him, for his eyelids fluttered. He smiled, though his eyes were heavy. "Good piloting," he whispered. "Send the message."

She pressed a kiss to his lips, and he opened his mouth and met her tongue. "One of these days," he whispered, "we're going to do lots of that."

"I can hardly wait."

"Me too." He fell back to sleep.

Sabralia followed the instructions he had left her and sent the message.

Chapter Seven

THE COM RECEIVED A message from Katherine Hub about payment procedures. She chose the option of setting an account up at the Hub financial dept, and arranged for transportation to the finance center and back to the ship in three hours. That gave her time to get a grav chair for Kaistril, and sell some jewels.

"Take a hot tube to go get the grav chair. I'll go with you to the jewelers, and carry the weapons." Kaistril's speech was more normal, but he still sat back against the chair with very little movement. Sabralia reluctantly opened the weaponry cabinet and armed herself with two small weapons, both non-lethal.

Sabralia had to go by herself to get a grav chair, for which she used an ordinary credit film from Alfyt's bag. As Sabralia got into the transport she summoned, she saw several young men looking at her. Her heart revved up. Were they going to rush her? Try to steal her goods? Or kidnap her? Before her imagination could get out of control, she grabbed one of her hot tubes, tilted her chin, and gave them a defiant look, making sure the young men could see she was armed. They did not move toward her.

The Hub was crazy with movement, chaotic. People on small gliders zipped around larger, slower transports, and moving pathways crisscrossed the entire interior of the Hub. The sphere-shaped center was full of buildings built on floating rafts or platforms built on jutting arms and scaffolding from the sphere wall. Balconies jutted from the sphere wall. Large door panels led to the spiral arms where ships docked.

It looked like mass confusion to Sabralia. She had not seen this part of the Hub when she traveled from her homeworld to Sirn's Harem; she had simply transferred ships out on the perimeter docks.

Sabralia gasped as a small group of people leaped off a walkway into the open sphere. They were wearing some sort of floater device, which they used to float on over to another walkway.

"What are they wearing, to float like that?" "Jack boots," the driver told her. "Very popular here with residents. Cheap. They hold a charge for a short while, but the charge can be replaced by movement."

She entered a personal transport shop with no incident and picked a grav chair with a riding platform on the back. It had two sets of controls that either she or Kaistril could use. Being raised as royalty did have some positive effects. She seemed to have an attitude that commanded respect. The proprietor of the shop not only summoned a transport that would take her privately back to the ship with her grav chair, but also paid for it.

When she entered the ship, she was surprised to see Kaistril dressed in some of Alfyt's more somber clothing, including a coat with a long hood that shaded his face. "Get me weapons," he said.

She took far more weapons out of the cabinet than she could ever imagine using. Kaistril had her place them in Alfyt's bags and lock them in the storage compartment under the chair. The cyborg appliances were in another bag he insisted she tuck in the storage area, too.

"We'll sell a small portion of the jewels and see how that works. If we show the whole collection, we might be noticed. We're three days ahead of the ships that are following us. Might have time to sell ship."

Sabralia chose several sets of fine jewelry, leaving the rarest and most expensive in the bag, which they locked up with the weapons.

They found a jeweler who asked no questions. Kaistril found nothing unusual about that. He was alert for the trade, but afterwards fell asleep in the transport she hired. The financial appointment was held in private and was over quickly. The credits she held were universal and easy to pass at any hub or port, and most larger cities. While there, she paid for the Hub news to be sent to her personal com.

It was so much easier than she'd expected. Her account was bonded to their fingerprints, and a universal credit stick slid neatly into her com. "Back to the ship?" she asked Kaistril, who's eyes were closed under the deep rim of the hood. He looked fragile, with blue hollows under his eyes.

"No. We should find a room."

While he rested in the chair, Sabralia found a rental agency. "We require a decent lodging," she had told one of the agents, "but we want something quiet. We are not interested in luxury accommodations or gaming resorts or intoxicant saloons in the area."

The agent set up the appointment and gave her coordinates to a building quite away from the heavily-populated center of the Hub, and ordered a private transport to carry her and Kaistril's chair to the building. Kaistril did not wake up as she moved him into the private transport, and she held his hand as they zipped and lurched through the bustling Hub.

The rental unit was built into the Hub wall, far from the busy floating platform area that filled the center. A concierge showed her the room, while Kaistril remained in the transport. Sabralia liked it. Tiny, smaller than the stateroom on the ship, it had a narrow balcony that overlooked a courtyard full of light and greenery. She paid the fee, and the driver helped unload the grav chair while she helped Kaistril into the room. She paid the concierge a generous tip.

She woke Kaistril up after the concierge left them alone.

"This is good," Kaistril said. "Until my brothers come..." He was exhausted, she could tell. She helped him to the small bed, and sank down beside him. *I wonder how many brothers he has? Or does he mean military brothers?*

The activity of selling the jewels and leaving the ship wore Kaistril out. He slept for most of the next twenty-four hours and continued to sleep almost constantly the next few days. Sabralia stayed inside the small apartment.

"The Hub is full of Sirn's sympathizers," Kaistril said in one of his brief moments of consciousness. "Order what you want for delivery. Get concierge to accept deliveries."

Daveed, the concierge, was willing to put her purchases on the apartment account, which she paid when he delivered the items she ordered. She was able to get food, clothes, anything they needed, while only leaving a payment record on the apartment account. She thought it might be a good idea if anyone was looking for them. They were lucky the Hub had no regular security force or methods for registering and tracking people.

Even with the jewel sales, Sabralia worried about their finances. Life on the Hub was expensive. She researched ship sales. What if Kaistril's brothers didn't arrive as quickly as he thought they would?

Kaistril continued to sleep heavily. Sabralia talked to him about the sale of the ship, but it had to be done soon, she thought, before their pursuers docked at the Hub. She placed an ad and then consulted Daveed for a safe place to meet potential buyers. Daveed and his wife had a small son. He ran the apartment complex while they saved money to immigrate to a world outside the war zone. Most of the apartment residents were sphere workers who needed affordable, safe housing. The ad brought in immediate responses. She chose to answer one that was politely worded, and made plans to meet at the Tea Room—a place Daveed strongly suggested.

The Tea Room was reassuring. Sabralia deposited her hot tubes in a safe that locked to her thumbprint and took a table away from the windows.

"I will be meeting someone. I am called Coloun," she told one of the servers, who promised to escort the potential buyer to her table. When the server left, she looked around.

The Tea Room had greenery and soothing colors of green, blue, and white. It served a wide range of beverages. She ordered a cup of spice tea and waited. Nerves made her stomach tight. She hoped this first meeting would bring a sale.

The server returned, escorting a small thin woman with short dark hair and warm brown skin to Sabralia's table. She wore a thick black quilted vest that fell below the knee and revealed wiry muscled bare arms.

"I am Coloun. Please join me."

The woman nodded in a formal manner and ordered a cup of roasted Kaf. "I am Tulse Vittorine."

Sabralia took a sip from her spice and fumbled with her com. "I can beam the specs to you."

Tulse Vittorine studied the specs while Sabralia studied her. This was no sex worker or dancer, like the women of the harem. There was a scar on her arm and another on her eyebrow. She wore no ornamentation at all, or cosmetics. And she seemed to know a lot about ships, for she studied the specs for quite some time.

"Has any work been done on it recently?" Tulse asked.

"A tracer was successfully removed from under the hull."

"Is someone pursuing the ship? Is that why the trace was removed?"

Sabralia hesitated. Many buyers would walk away if they knew Sirn's men were following it. But she didn't want to lie and put the buyer in danger.

"The ship belonged to my husband. I received word he had been attacked by marauders and I fled here with a servant. I have not heard from my husband, so I assume the two ships that are following are not friends or colleagues. The ship is small but luxurious and in excellent shape."

"How far behind you were the pursuers?"

"They will not dock here for at least thirty-six hours."

"A buyer would have to move the vessel and pay for redocking, plus remove insignia from the hull. And change the ship's signature. All those are expensive procedures. Especially in a short amount of time."

"I would perhaps be willing to consider a counter offer, if I was assured that such procedures would indeed take place within thirty-six hours."

Tulse Vittorine tapped off the specs and stood. "I would like to see the ship."

"Of course. If you will follow my transport, I will give you a tour."

Sabralia was glad Kaistril had thought ahead, giving her a lock code for the ship's system. "You are more than welcome to explore. The system is locked, but I will provide the unlock code at the time of sale."

"Of course."

While Tulse checked the coms and disappeared into the lower level, Sabralia drifted to the stateroom. So many memories of Kaistril. Tears stung her eyes. This is over, our short time together.

Sabralia took a deep breath. Enough. She had a ship to sell.

When Tulse came back to the main com, Sabralia was ready. "If you purchase this ship and redock it, and change the ship's signature and hull insignia, I will give you a rebate of a hundred thousand credits upon proof of those actions."

Tulse agreed and they traveled to a credit station for the exchange. Afterwards, Sabralia beamed the unlock code to Tulse's com after verification of the credit transfer came through. "She is all yours now," she said when it was done. "Enjoy your ship."

Tulse Vittorine's face split into a gleaming smile, showing a mouthful of strong white teeth. It transformed her into a beauty, and Sabralia suddenly realized that Tulse was really quite young. "I will contact you in a few hours when the changes have been made."

Sabralia nodded. "I look forward to hearing from you."

She traveled back to the apartment and rushed inside. Kaistril was asleep and did not respond to her greeting. The activity of leaving the ship had worn him out. Surely a day's rest would give him more energy and alertness.

Tulse Vittorine contacted Sabralia twelve hours later, waking her from sleep. She had the proof of changes. Sabralia saved the data, then verified it through the Hub system. Yes, there it was, docked on a spiral far from the original one, with a new com signature and title. The Tulse Pulse. Cute.

Sabralia journeyed to a nearby credit station and transferred the required credit to Tulse. Her sense of relief was huge. The ship was moved and changed. Their pursuers would have a much harder time finding them, especially if Tulse left the Hub in a few days. The Hub required no record of their transaction, only Tulse and Sabralia knew of it.

"So dangerous, Sabra," Kaistril said when she told him about the sale.

"I was cautious, Kaistril. And we might need the credits if your brothers are delayed somehow."

"The signature and hull insignia are changed?"

"Yes. I double checked through the Hub system." She showed him the proof and he was satisfied.

"You did well, Sabra. This gives us a greater degree of safety. And it is good to be prepared in case my brothers don't show up on time."

She knew he felt bad about being so helpless. "We'll be fine now. We just need to wait." Wait for you to get better, she wanted to say.

Since they didn't leave their small room, there was nothing to do but sleep, or watch the Hub com.

"He seems honest," Kaistril said of Daveed during one of his short alert periods.

"I do think he is honest," Sabralia agreed. "He lives next door with his wife and three small children. She does not speak Standard well, but we have exchanged greetings and a few words. They plan to emigrate to Yonder."

Yonder was a world newly opened for colonization, far out on the Rim, away from the war.

Kaistril talked to Daveed and arranged for him to be a courier with a sale of more jewels. Daveed's wife, Amira, confided that with the courier fee Kaistril paid, they nearly had enough for a colonization package. Amira invited her over daily while her young ones napped, for tea. She also taught Sabralia a type of lace making, something to while away the time while Kaistril slept.

"It is so sad your husband so sick. Very sad. You see doctor?" Amira's big brown eyes were full of concern.

Sabralia brought up the idea of seeing a doctor to Kaistril, who was getting too thin and far too tired. He slept constantly except for brief moments, and when he did eat he just took a few bites, and then he'd be off to sleep again. "It's not right, Kaistril. You should be feeling better, shouldn't you?"

"We'll wait until my brothers get here. I trust their ship's doctor more than I would trust a physician here. They might recognize that cyborg applications were on me, alert someone. No records, we can't be found."

"Do you think someone is looking for us?"

"Maybe for us. Maybe for the ship. They might know who we are. I have no way of knowing what kind of security might have been running at the Sirn's spaceport..." His voice got weaker as he spoke. "There might be visuals."

Sabralia thought about that. "If there were visuals, then they know you are a former cyborg, and they probably know about the failsafe."

One day, Daveed came to the door, his dark eyes huge. "Sabralia, there is some news you should know. Someone has been visiting different lodgings, asking for information. Two dark-haired Puregen men have been found dead...murdered."

"I see." Her heart pounded in panic.

"I thought you should know because your man is a dark-haired Puregen. Don't open your door. And you should order security barriers for your door."

She did so, and Daveed installed them.

"Good. Good... family will be here soon," Kaistril said when he saw the security barriers, which strengthened the doorway locks and alerted them to any movement near their room. Daveed had promised to keep an eye out for trouble. The courtyard was secure, so Sabralia could still enjoy the balcony and visits with Amira.

"How can they be here so soon? New Prague is two systems away."

"Yes. But secret...have a jump line."

A jump line, an anomaly that pulled a ship through space at speeds unachievable by space flight. Like a current running through space.

"New Prague has a jump line?"

"Yes. But it's a secret. Or Sirn..."

He didn't need to finish. Sirn was acquiring jump lines wherever he could.

Sabralia checked the com over and over for news of the murders. She knew she was acting strangely. Knowing someone was out there, perhaps looking for Kaistril, made her jittery, but exhausted. Nothing tasted good.

Kaistril was in the small bed, bare from the waist up. He was sleeping, like always, and curled into himself. She missed the Kaistril she'd just started to know, and she missed the physical closeness she'd had with him as her cyborg. The days of warm baths, of arms holding her, stroking her as she fell to sleep, were gone. The memories of the heated passion they shared seemed almost like a dream now.

Chapter Eight

THE MESSAGE CAME THREE days later, just as Sabralia was beginning to feel desperate. Two more dark-haired men had been killed, their gruesome stories played constantly once the Hub news-view cast. She made sure the weapons were nearby at all times. Kaistril couldn't defend himself, it was up to her.

She replied to the message, "Kaistril is ill. I can get him to your ship. He can walk a short distance. There is a difficulty—someone may be searching for us. They have our descriptions. Several men matching Kaistril's description have been killed in the past few days."

"Give me your location. We will come directly to your lodging for you. Be ready." The message was signed as Commander Kyler. She woke Kaistril up and got him dressed to go.

"Kyler is coming here to the lodging for us."

"Good, that will make it safer."

To her surprise, Kaistril called for Daveed to join them.

When he did, Kaistril tapped an amount onto Daveed's com and completed the transaction with his thumbprint. "Here. You have been very kind to my wife and myself. I hope you and your wife have the luck of the Star Gods in your new world." Daveed stared at the com. "That is far more than I need."

"I know, but I thank you. Your family deserves to be off this Hub, somewhere safe. Where will you go?"

"Yonder. Free land on that planet, good farmland on two continents with little mining. Mixed immigration and immigrant constitutions, too, to protect the colonists. A good place to raise a family."

Kaistril nodded. "If you should change your mind, come to New Prague. We are sparsely populated, with most of the population concentrated on the east coast of one continent. We have an open constitution, not Puregen." He tapped his com

"My personal contact."

"We will research New Prague," Daveed said.

"I wish you and your wife well," Sabralia told him, tears pricking her eyes. Daveed and Amira were the closest people she'd had for friends in many years.

"And I you."

Kaistril dozed while they waited, the bags packed and ready. The door alarm buzzed and the security screen showed a tall, dark-haired man. Sabralia shook Kaistril awake, then opened the door at Kaistril's nod. The man resembled Kaistril, but his eyes were silver gray. And he was huge, a head taller than Kaistril, and wide, his shoulders grazing the doorway.

"Kyler. Good you're here, you monster." Kaistril tried to stand, and Sabralia rushed to his side to help him.

"What is wrong with him?" The man's voice was sharp.

"Failsafe," Kaistril said. "She had to remove the implants."

"Implants?" Kyler skewered her with his eyes.

"Cyborg implants," Sabralia answered.

"All on the com. Info." Kaistril indicated the bag.

Kyler snatched it. "Move out."

Other men were with him, dressed in black, form-fitting uniforms, with silver and red markings on their chests and shoulders. The men grabbed Kaistril by the arms and pulled him swiftly into a small transport. Sabralia followed, awkward with her thick cloak and bag.

Everything happened so fast. While the transport maneuvered to the New Prague ship, Kyler barked orders into a com, to someone named Karvar. He uploaded Kaistril's com. Sabralia sagged against her seat in relief. There was a medic on board, someone who could help Kaistril. Tears pricked her eyes. He was already asleep, several seats in front of her, slumped limply with his head against the wall. Medics greeted them in the docking bay. One was tall, with dark hair and thick lashes surrounding amber eyes. He wore focals. Another brother?

"Take the woman to quarters on level four," Kyler commanded. His silver eyes slid over her, making her feel cold. For some reason he didn't like her, she could tell. "Run her through our system, Security One priority."

Two soldiers escorted her to a lift, and then down to a small room. They politely asked for her thumbprint and a retinal scan. "A meal will be brought in two hours," one soldier said afterwards.

"I want to be with Kaistril. Isn't there somewhere I can wait, while he is examined?"

"Commander Kyler will take care of his brother. It is best you stay here, out of the way."

Sabralia was left alone in a small room. The room was stark and chilly, and the narrow bunk was hard. It looked like a prison cell, with the hygenie right in the same room. On impulse she tried the door. She was locked in.

Worrying about Kaistril made her feel sick. She wished someone would come with information. She found a common com and tried it. "This is Sabralia. I came with Kaistril. Can someone inform me what is happening? Is Kaistril all right?"

She repeated the message several times before she got an anonymous response.

"We will be leaping to Goldshawk Hub in thirty hours. Commander Kaistril is stabilized and recovering. He requires rest before we leap. Please follow the procedures broadcast prior to the jump to ensure your safety."

He was well. That was all that mattered. "May I see him before we jump?" There was a pause, then a reply. Sabralia would be summoned for a brief visit before the jump.

Relieved, she ate the cold, unappetizing food, and bathed in a daze. Finally, she dozed for a while, until an announcement for the jump woke her.

"SHE IS FROM COLOUN, in fourth sector. It is an agricultural world and supplies Sirn's forces. She was married to Sirn in a treaty contract." Karvar read the information to Kyler.

"A treaty wife."

"Yes."

"Is she important enough for Sirn to come after? Because we have reports that they were being sought by Sirn's forces," Kyler said.

"According to the woman, Sirn was overthrown recently, at his palace."

"Perhaps. But his forces are on the move again, so whether he is in charge, or his successor, they seem to have the same agenda."

"We should have insider news soon," Karvar said. "They may be after the woman for some reason. Perhaps she has some knowledge she shouldn't have."

"Perhaps. Still, if there was a coup, as she maintains, she might have been able to find some delicate information." Kyler drummed his fingers on the com. "I will allow her to visit Kaistril, and while she is with him, I will have her belongings searched."

Karvar nodded. "Good."

"I am also making arrangements to get her off-ship. I am not taking her to New Prague. If she remains with Kaistril, she would have access to the entire Governing Body. Including Mother. She is too high a security risk."

"Do you think Kaistril wants her to come with us?" Karvar asked. "Kaistril has never been interested in keeping any woman around for long. As long as she is safe, he'll be fine with it. We'll send her back to Coloun."

Karvar nodded.

"I'll have two ensigns escort her to a ship that will take her to her homeworld." Kyler checked info on the com. "There is a transport out in two days' time. Meanwhile, she will remain in her quarters under watch."

Relief flooded through Sabralia. They were not trying to keep her away from Kaistril. Maybe she could stay with him now, instead of in that ugly room.

Kaistril was stretched under a white coverlet in a medic room. He was asleep, but his coloring was good, and the hollows below his cheek bones were gone. The medic with the focals was in attendance. He looked remarkably like Kaistril, but with amber eyes under the lenses, and his hair was dark reddish brown, not black.

"I am Karvar, Kaistril's brother and physician."

"Oh. I did not know he had a second brother on this ship."

"Yes, Kyler is our brother also."

"Kaistril is going to be all right?"

"Yes. We removed the implant inside his skull that fed the nanos, and we cleared all the nanos out of his bloodstream. He should wake in the next few hours."

"Wonderful. I was so worried." She bent over the bed and stroked Kaistril's corded hair. He looked so good, healthy. His color was fine, and there were no blue shadows under his crescent eyelashes. Sabralia continued stroking his hair and held his hand, speaking now and then of nothing important.

"I'm so glad your brother was able to remove the implant and clean out the nanos. I know you are going to be fine."

She held his limp hand to her cheek and brushed kisses against his palm. "Soon you will be awake and strong."

What am I going to do? She was completely in love with him. At least he would be healthy. And with his family.

Karvar reappeared, and she pressed a kiss on Kaistril's cheek. "Sleep well," she whispered.

As the men escorted her back to the lonely, utilitarian room, she struggled not to cry. She loved him. Real love, the kind that lasted a lifetime. Locked back into the ugly room, she cried hard, gulping sobs. Kaistril would live...he would get better...he had a full life with a family to return to. Maybe there was even a woman, back on New Prague, some strong athletic Puregen...

Was there any place for her in his new life? Did he even have good memories of her? She'd been his mistress, while he'd been a slave cyborg...that couldn't hold good memories for him. She must remind him of his captivity.

But the ship. Sabralia was sure his memories of their time together on the ship were pleasant. She knew he enjoyed the intimate sexual interludes...but for her it had been life-changing. She would never forget. For her, it had been lovemaking, not just for the pure carnal pleasure, but for the soft look in his light blue eyes after he came, the warm arms that held her without a command. But did he want her in his real life?

Chapter Nine

A SUMMONS AT HER DOOR awoke her. She sat up, full of hope that Kaistril would be awake and alert soon.

However, two soldiers entered her small room.

"Pack the items you want to take with you," one of them said.

"Take with me? Where?"

"We are moving you to a nonmilitary transport. It is safer." Confused, Sabralia packed the few items she had placed around the room into her bag. Safer than a military transport?

"Is Kaistril going to be on this transport, too?"

"I do not know. He is still under the doctor's care and may follow when he is stronger. Our orders are to get you out safely."

"It will be more comfortable for a lady, than on a military ship," the other soldier said.

That might well be true, if the rest of this ship was anything like this room.

The men escorted her off-ship to a small transport. From there, they flew away to a dock across the Hub.

One soldier got out to arrange her departure. When he returned, they walked her to a glide path that moved them toward a loading dock.

The walkway was full of people and even a few herds of farm animals in transport container fields. People were talking all around them, and Sabralia was shocked to hear the language of her homeworld. She turned to the people speaking it.

"You are from Coloun?" she asked in a low voice.

"Yes, miss. We are returning to Coloun with breeding stock."

"This ship is going to Coloun?"

"Of course."

Anger filled her. They were sending her away from Kaistril. Back to her home world, where Sirn could find her, where Sirn ruled. She turned her face away slowly, trying not to show her emotion to the escort.

Along the walkway were small booths and portable merchant stands. Several held the Jack boots and glider boards that were so popular with Hub people.

She had credits, left over from the ship's sale, and she knew they would work with just a thumbprint.

She just needed to lose the escort.

Two young men with a stack of glider boards were near the walkway and she would soon pass them. She caught their eyes and smiled, wiggling a finger to get one to come close. "Get me off this glide path and away from these two soldiers, and I will pay a triple price for a glider," she said to them, in her home language. *I hope they understand.*

The boys' faces burst into smiles. "Certainly, miss," one spoke in Coloun.

"Where to, miss?"

"Farther down. These men I'm with are forcing me onto the ship. I don't want to go. But I don't know how to run a glider or the boots. Could you carry me down a couple levels? And show me how they work? I'll pay you." She spoke quickly. One of the guards was starting to frown.

"Sure. We get it." Sabralia turned away and walked with her escort several paces, until the two boys suddenly grabbed her on both sides, and yanked her off the path. She screamed as they dropped—she thought they would hit bottom. However, the boys' gliders suddenly burst on, and they floated down several levels, finally landing in a crowded plaza, full of eateries and other businesses, clogged with customers. Far above she could hear the angry shouts of her escort, and she grinned.

The glider wasn't that hard to use, it already held an energy charge, while the boots would have to be moved to rev up. She chose a glider with a narrow hand stick for direction. Then, after paying the boys well and practicing with the glider, she took off to a mid-section plaza, this one very large.

The soldiers would look for her, she thought. Her bright blue floral cloak would be easy enough to spot. She found a clothing store and covered her fashionable floral cloak with a dark brown one. On impulse, she ducked into a small tea shop after seeing several women at the windows. Soldiers would not think about looking for her there, she was sure. While drinking a cup of spice, accompanied by a plate of sweet buns, she asked general questions about the Hub from her server, a kind-faced older woman. By the time she left, she had coordinates for a safe, but modest, sleeping inn. Some hours later, after she arrived to her safe, tiny room, she tried to decide what to do.

Kaistril hadn't sent her away, it was his brothers—that bossy Kyler and that scary silent brother with the hair all slicked back, and the focals...they wanted her out of Kaistril's life.

Sirn might still be alive, she'd heard that rumor. Perhaps that was why they'd sent her away. She was still a married woman. But Kaistril said she could be divorced by New Prague law. Or maybe their information wasn't current and they didn't know about the coup...maybe they thought she was loyal to Sirn.

Sabralia couldn't think of anything else to do except wait for the guards to quit looking for her. Kaistril...a tear slipped down her cheek. He would be all right. His brothers did care about him, even if they were unkind to her.

Her credits would last for a long while. There was enough to get on a transport to anywhere. Not to Coloun, though. If Sirn was alive, harboring her would be a death sentence for her cousin. Not that Sirn cared. It was just a matter of pride.

She could take a transport to New Prague. From there perhaps she could get a message to Kaistril, letting him know where she was.

Daveed had his personal contact information!

She left her cubicle and took a transport toward Daveed's apartments. Daveed and Amira we surprised to see her. They were packing in preparation for their journey to Yonder.

She left them, with full contact information, then searched for transport packages to Yonder. She stayed up long past her sleep cycle, researching various immigration packages, trying to decide what would work for her. Many came with a skilled training course. She would definitely need one of those, since she had no life skills. A transport to Yonder would be boarding in three days. It might even be the same one Daveed and his family was on. She could hide from the New Prague Military until then. At least they were easy to see in their uniforms.

I will probably never see him again. There was war and more war, and she would be on a remote world, sewing tough work clothing for farmers, or growing herbs for harvest. Kaistril would be with his Tier fighting for freedom. Right before she left the Hub she would beam a message to him through the Hub's system, so someday he would be sure to receive it, telling him where she was going.

It was a long time until she slept.

KAISTRIL AWOKE IN A medbed. It took a moment before he remembered Kyler and Karvar. He was on his way home. He stood up, expecting to feel weak and dizzy, but he felt great.

Karvar suddenly burst into the room. "You're awake. How do you feel?"

"Great. Not dizzy. Normal. I probably lost some muscle mass, but that will return."

Karvar smiled. "Since I'm not familiar with the appliances you wore, we were worried."

"Where's Sabralia?" He could hardly wait to see her. He could hardly wait to get her alone...

Karvar pushed up his focals and Kaistril frowned. That was a nervous sign...

"Well, the thing is, Kyler decided...I decided too, that she should return to her home planet. She is Sirn's wife, you know. A security risk."

Kyler joined them.

"She's one of Sirn's wives. He has dozens. And Sirn's probably dead. There was a coup at his pleasure palace. We managed to escape." Kaistril frowned at them. Fury roared through him. They'd sent her away, into danger?

"She mentioned something about a fight or something."

"You didn't ask her about what happened?" Kaistril stared at his larger brother in disbelief.

"No. We were concerned about getting you stabilized."

Kaistril raised an eyebrow. "Really? You attended Karvar in the surgery to remove the appliance inside my head?"

"Well, no, but..." His voice trailed off.

"So, what did you talk to her about?"

"I didn't talk to her, all right? We ran a bio on her. We knew she was married to Sirn. I figured she was a security risk. Then we searched her belongings and found films. Dozens of them, with Sirn's Forces' encryption."

"I knew they were there. We were bringing them to you, you idiots."

"We thought she might send information back to Sirn."

"Seriously? How does that make any sense! About what? A cyborg getting appliances removed? That she had a lot of his high-tech military secrets?" Kaistril shook his head in disgust. "So find me a transport to Coloun. I'll meet up with her there."

Kyler and Karvar exchanged quick glances.

"What?"

Kyler took a deep breath. "She didn't make it onto the transport. Apparently, she paid a couple glider vendors to glide her off the walkway. The escorts I sent didn't have floaters on. She got away."

Kaistril burst out laughing. "My plump little queen outwitted your ensigns?" He stared them down for a moment, then knew what he had to do. "I want my cyborg appliances. Right now."

Karvar looked confused. He pushed his focals back up his nose.

"They are in my lab. I wanted to look at them."

"Get them. And get me some quick food and clothes. Not a uniform." Then he turned to Kyler. "So do you have soldiers out looking for her?"

"Yes. But it appears she has many credits, enough to rent a room and find different clothing."

"Of course she has plenty. We sold half of the harem's jewels and a state of the art luxury cruiser." Karvar came back with a tray holding the cyborg appliances.

"So you got that inner piece out?" Kaistril asked.

"Yes. We also ran your blood through a filtering process to clean out the nanos that were keeping you asleep."

"Good." Kaistril grabbed the temple appliance and went to a small mirror over a lav.

"Well, study up those films, little brother. From what I could see, they hold most of Sirn's campaign notes, cyborg mechanics and weaponry specs." As he spoke, Kaistril activated the temple appliance and slapped it onto his head.

"I can find her with these appliances. They are keyed to her." He pushed the arm com on over the neatly healed wound and did the same with the thigh appliance. Their lights flashed as the appliances grounded themselves in his body. It didn't even hurt that much. Data poured into his mind. Just like old times. Only not. Now they would serve his purposes, he wouldn't be serving theirs. He smiled.

"I need clothes. Not a uniform. Now!"

"What are you doing? Are you crazy?"

Kaistril raised an eyebrow at his little brother. "You removed the remainder of the failsafe and the nanos, right?"

"Y-Yes," Karvar sputtered.

"Then it's all right." He searched data on his arm com. "Since you idiots lost my woman in the sphere, I'm going to go find her. With my appliances, I can track her. I need my weapons, too."

"We wanted to research those," Kyler protested.

"Then some of your weapons." Kaistril's words were clipped. He was losing what little patience he owned. If he wasn't so glad to see his brothers, he would have pounded them by now. Putting Sabralia in danger, alone in a hub!

He looked up at his astonished brother. "I want those items now. If I don't get them in five minutes, I'm leaving without them. You can tell Maman that you let me go out into a Hub with no weapons."

"I'll get some men to accompany you," Kyler said.

"No thanks. If I get close and she sees your men, she might take off. You didn't exactly make her feel welcome, did you? It will be quicker if I go alone."

"I've got clothes you can wear," Karvar said.

Karvar left and returned with a small bag of clothing. Kaistril dressed in New Prague clothing—syntho skin leggings, a blue tunic of brushed cloth, and a wide belt that held several compartments. Karvar had the knee-high boots of treated eth skin, which molded to his feet just right. "I'd forgotten how good it felt to be dressed like a Protectorate," he said. "It is good."

"You look fine."

Afterwards, they led Kaistril to the dock, trying to dissuade him the whole time. Giving up, Kyler offered him a small blaster and a small credit stick.

"Don't need the stick, I have lots of credits. Got a floater vest?"

What if she decided to hop some transport to somewhere? Surely she wouldn't do anything crazy. Hopefully she's holed up somewhere, expecting to hear from me. He tapped a message to her.

He hadn't purchased a transmitter code for this sphere, so the transmission wouldn't go though. He wondered if Sabralia knew you had to buy a transmitter code unless you were calling a local business. There were so many things she didn't know, going from her agricultural homeworld to Sirn's Harem. The sooner he found her, the better. "I'll take your credits after all."

After Kaistril left the ship, he searched for her signal. The sphere had many areas where magnetism interfered with his signal search, and he would need to be quite close to her in distance to find her. This could take some time. He found a small glider that would move him faster than his float vest and headed for a Hub station where he could get a transmitter code.

"I'm coming with you." Kyler was dressed in non-military clothing.

"Yes, because she won't possibly recognize you without your uniform." Kaistril felt sarcastic, still put out with their highhanded behavior.

"I'll stay back."

"Good."

"Her signal is weak. I have to be within a mile to register her. That was never a problem in the Harem. Here, it could take awhile." He got access to the Hub com and tried to contact her, but she didn't answer her com. She probably thought Kyler and Karvar were trying to get in touch.

Several hours later, Kaistril located her signal on a large plaza in the midsection of the sphere. It was crowded with vendors, traders, small hoppers, and youngsters on gliders and floats.

He looked for her floral cloak, but didn't see it. She probably covered it with something drab.

Then...he found her.

Sabralia was tucked into the side of a tiny eatery, which seemed relatively quiet. She was wearing a dull brown cloak over her floral one, just as he suspected, and she'd had her hair done in an elaborate coiffure of tiny braids and ribbons. She also wore face paint, quite heavy. She looked different, pretty in an exotic way, older and more sophisticated. Good disguise.

"Sabra," he called. She looked up and her eyes opened wide.

"Kaistril? Are you all right?" She flew toward him, and then she was in his arms, soft and sweet. Right where she was supposed to be, and he was never letting her go again.

He laughed, relieved she was safe. "I'm great. Better than ever. You look wonderful. I was worried about you alone on the Hub."

"I'm fine. I didn't think I'd ever see you again." Her eyes were bright with unshed tears.

He pressed his lips to hers, anxious to taste her, threading one hand into her expensive coiffure. Her arms slid tight around his neck and her mouth was as hungry as his. He slid his hands slowly down her back to her bottom, cupped her, and pulled her up tight against his already hard cock, so the juncture of her fit over his swollen member.

He grinned. "Come. We'll take a transport to the ship."

She giggled again.

They walked with arms around each other to a small dock.

"Are you wearing these so you could find me?" She tapped on his arm com.

"Yes. You can't hide from me when I have these on." He pressed a swift kiss on her lips. "My brothers are idiots, but they'll figure it out. Don't worry about any of that."

"I'll bet they were shocked when you put the appliances back on."

He nodded. "Yes. But I do like the enhanced capabilities they give me. Quite a good addition for a warrior."

A transport docked, and as they turned to enter, the door slid open on several men in white uniforms who held small blasters pointed at them.

Sabralia froze, but Kaistril yanked her off the platform into a fall, while blasters fired all around them.

"Float!" he yelled as they dropped, and their fall slowed as the vest activated.

After they descended down, Kaistril dragged her behind a strut, and then they were both sliding down it.

The transport couldn't move as swiftly as they did and the soldiers had no floaters on.

"Under here." He pulled them under a walkway, close to the top, so they were hidden from view. "We're gong to slide across the top here, then try to get to that plaza." He indicated a very busy plaza. The transport was on the other side of the walkway. It would have to cross a busy transport route to get to the plaza, which was jammed with transports, hoppers, and people on floaters and glide rides.

"They are up there. Hurry."

They rushed toward the plaza, and threaded through transports and people, finally entering a crowded store.

"We'll be much harder to track on foot. Except..." He paused.

"Except what?"

"If they are from Sirn, they could have your id chip code."

She swallowed hard. "I have a chip?"

"A small one. It only transmits a short distance, so I thought it was benign. I should have taken it out. They must have more sensitive equipment than I do. It took me forever to find you." He took a deep breath and hugged her tight. "At least I found you first. We'll be all right. I think if we follow this down we can take one of the high-speed glides."

They took a down glide. Far above her she thought she saw the uniformed men.

Kaistril was speaking into his com. "We're taking the zed level glide. A transport from the ship should meet us. They'll be well-armed. We need a medic."

They hurtled across the sphere on a fast glide and Kaistril watched for his brother's and the soldiers. A transport, larger than most that flew through the interior of the Hub, pulled right up to them, scattering gliders and pedestrians. Kaistril grabbed her under the arms and pushed her toward the open door. Strong hands grabbed her and Kaistril clambered on after her.

Kyler, looking angry and frightening, asked, "Are they following her code or her appearance?"

Kaistril looked at his com. "Both, actually. Her code is scrambled here. Too many magnetic fields in the area."

"Go. Trouble." Kyler barked to the pilot

Kaistril practically dragged her to a seat.

"Strap down." That was Karvar, who was also in the transport.

Sabralia strapped herself into a harness with fumbling fingers. What now?

The transport took off, braking and speeding through the traffic with nauseating speed. Sabralia shut her eyes, waiting for a collision.

"Here, this will do." The transport pulled into a small, empty loading dock. Karvar leaped out of his seat and approached Sabralia with a med bag.

"We need to get that chip out, Sabralia," Kaistril said. "I think they know we have the films. Or suspect it. We need to get them back to New Prague. They will be a great help."

Karvar cleared his throat, then turned to Kaistril. "I thought I could remove the id chip here in the transport. Then we can get her onto the ship and off-hub without being detected."

"Good plan." Kaistril got out of his seat. "I'll hold your hand, Sabra. Karvar can give you an anesthetic so it doesn't hurt."

Karvar popped a capsule under her nose, and she got dizzy immediately.

"It is in your upper arm, did you know?" She shook her head.

"I knew, but I thought its signal was so weak it wouldn't matter, so I didn't remove it while we were on the ship." Kaistril lifted her arm and pulled up the loose sleeve of her dress. He showed her a tiny hard spot on the back of her upper arm, something she'd never noticed before.

"Hold her still." Karvar pressed a small device against the spot. She felt nothing. They applied a newskin over the small wound.

"Commander, we have been detected. Shall I begin evasive maneuvers?" the pilot asked.

"Affirmative."

The brothers leaped back into their seats, and the transport took off with a jerky, hard turn. Weapon fire rained upon them for a short burst.

"Head for a busy plaza!" Kaistril barked. "I can jump with the emitter, lose it, then return to New Prague on public transport. You get Sabralia to the ship and get off-hub."

"Public transport? Why don't we just lose the chip and all leave together?" Kyler protested.

"The chip has to be kept at body temperature, or they'll know it has been detected."

Kyler snorted. "Give it to me. You're still underweight and need your rest, you idiot."

"You're right." Kaistril smiled. "I'd rather be with Sabra, anyway, to make sure you two don't think up some other stupid scheme."

"Sorry, Kaistril. And you, too, Sabralia," Karvar, cheeks red, held a small tube to Kyler's arm and struck a button. He then sealed the small wound. "Just dig it out with your knife when you want to. It's shallow."

"Here's your credit stick," Kaistril shoved the small device into Kyler''s hand and he slid it into his com.

"Give me your cloak," Kyler said to Sabralia. She shrugged it off and he threw it over his clothing. It looked ridiculous, being far too small, with feminine ruffles along the bottom edge.

"Don't say a word," Kyler said to his brothers with a scowl. The ship jerked to a halt and Kyler leaped out the door into a thick crowd below, the cloak flapping. "Go!" he shouted as they pulled up.

Two levels up, as Sirn's men followed Kyler down several levels, they all left the transport at a trade station and scattered into several small transports. "Do some sightseeing, return to the ship in a couple hours or so." Kaistril said.

Chapter Ten

SABRALIA COULDN'T KEEP her hands off Kaistril, and he didn't seem to mind, pulling her into doorways and along the side of buildings for kisses. Her heart was full of delight at being with him, at his health and vitality, so different than when she'd last seen him.

"I explained everything to my brothers. They thought you were a security risk."

"What did you tell them?"

"That you were my woman." He pressed a hard kiss to her lips and she melted against him, blood churning. "I wish we could be alone," Kaistril whispered into her ear. "We have nearly an hour before we need to grab a transport."

Sabralia slid her hands up his chest, relishing the feel of his hard body under her fingers. "Come with me. I have a room. Plus, I want to get my belongings." She dragged him by the hand to her micro sleep room a few plazas away.

Last night she had cried herself to sleep, thinking she might never see him again, and now he was here with her, healthy, vigorous. And he couldn't keep his hands off her, either.

He wrapped his arms around her as they moved on a walkway, and tapped on his arm com. "I'm letting them know we have some important things to do, so we'll be there when we get there."

"So we don't have to rush?"

He pulled her in front of him so her back rested against him, with his arms wrapped around, his lips at the soft skin of her nape. "No rushing. We need to celebrate."

They made it to her room, quickly. There was barely room for both of them to stand on the small floor space in front of her bunk. "You lay down first. I went shopping and I was thinking about you. I want you to see what I bought," Sabralia said.

Kaistril tossed his clothing onto the floor and stretched on the tiny bunk. Sabralia took off her dark blue gown, and the long pantaloons under it, all the while enjoying the sight of his long lean body on the small bunk. He was already hard, his length standing up proud.

Next to her skin, she wore a pink fuzzy sheath, some type of stretchy, fuzzy lace. It cupped her breasts, forming deep cleavage. It had a slit opening at the crotch.

"That is amazing," he said.

"I bought several. Some have leggings. They are designed to keep you warm. I thought they would be nice in the colonies."

Kaistril sat up and pulled her to him so his face was right in her cleavage. "You're not going to the colonies."

"No?" she asked softly.

"No. You are coming home with me. You'll share my quarters on the ship, and you'll share my rooms at my mother's palace."

"Palace?" Her voice squeaked and Kaistril chuckled, dragging her on top of him so his erection was trapped against her soft stomach covered in the silky fuzzy lace.

"I guess I forgot to tell you my mother is the Protectorate of New Prague."

His hands were gliding softly up and down her backside, drawing tingling circles on her bottom.

"Well, that actually explains a lot." She feathered her lips against his silky chest hair, reveling in the texture.

"She'll annul your marriage to Sirn."

Sabralia smiled. "He won't know where I am, anyway."

"But I can't marry you legally unless you are free of him."

Sabralia sat up in shock. "You want to marry me? I thought you wanted to go back to your Tier."

His hands cupped her breasts in the silky fuzz. "Not anymore. Now I want to settle in New Prague with my lovely wife and consult with our military. I'm an expert on Sirn's Cyborgs."

"A real marriage? No harem? Children?"

"Yes, just you and our young. But I'll bake the sweet buns. I'm a better cook."

Tears filled her eyes and he pulled her down and kissed them away.

"I love you, Sabra. I want us to be together. I want the life we can build together."

She sighed. "That's what I want, also."

With a groan, Kaistril rolled her onto her back. "Want to be inside," he whispered as his lips trailed along her neck. "It's been too long."

"No more waiting," she agreed, wrapping her legs around his hips, welcoming his rigid flesh with equal urgency.

He slid into her in a hard, urgent rush and she met him clutching him to her with her legs and pussy, enjoying his gasp of delight. She met his hard thrusts with undulations of her own, reveling in his strength, in the wild passion between them.

Later, as they took a private transport to the jump ship Kaistril tapped away on his com.

"Who are you contacting?" Sabralia asked. She was pleasantly exhausted.

"Daveed. Letting him know they can have free passage to New Prague and a waiver of immigration wait time if they join us right now. He says yes. Sending him the ship's location."

Sabralia smiled. Free passage and a waiver of wait time would make Daveed and Amira prosperous immigrants.

They got on board the New Prague ship. Kaistril took care of business, mainly concerning Daveed and his family, and then lead her to his room.

Karvar met them, but barely greeted them, his eyes glued to his com screen. "Your family suite is ready." He muttered. "Kyler still hasn't arrived back at the ship, though all his vitals showed normal on my screen."

"Do you think your brother is all right? They haven't caught him, have they?"

"No, the signal is good," Karvar said. "I wired a panic button that will pick up sounds, heart rate, all that. He seems fine."

"Kyler is probably having the time of his life zooming around the sphere," Kaistril said.

Karvar looked up from the com. "She's coming with us? Not traveling on?"

"She's going to be my wife."

"Oh." Karvar sighed. "Well, if you have a wife, and Kyler has agreed to marry the Chancellor's daughter, then mother's going to start arranging my marriage." He went back to the com, looking depressed. "Kellac found a woman, too."

"Life is tough, little brother," Kaistril said with a chuckle.

Back in their quarters—a small room with a comfortable bed and separate bathing area—Sabralia said, "Your mother might not think our marriage is such a great idea, since she believes in arranging marriages for her sons."

Kaistril snorted. "She can only suggest it. And why Kyler would go along with it I can't fathom. Probably something to do with Kellac and I disappearing. Kyler's the oldest. He always thinks he's responsible for everything. Trying to make some happy family memories, I suspect."

"Kellac is another brother?"

"Yes. He got imprisoned on a Puregen world. It's a long story. I don't even know the whole thing." Kaistril gathered her into his arms and yawned. "I'm not quite recovered yet. Karvar said I would need extra rest for a week or so. I think we'll have to spend most of the journey in bed." He grinned.

Sabralia slid into the comfortable bed with him and rained affectionate kisses over his face. "Your recovery is my number one priority."

The End

About The Author

BIO

Take a bookworm. Hand her a stack of her much older brother's Sci-fi and fantasy novels, thrillers and horror comics. Then introduce the world of romance.

Make her a jinx. Every great genre TV show she loves gets the ax! So often the romances have no happy ending. She gets upset about no romance in the world and writes her own stories with happy endings.

Throw this all together, shake constantly, and pour onto a computer keyboard.

There!

You have me,

Melisse Aires

Find me!

I have a newsletter! sendfox.com/melisseaires[1]

---

1. http://sendfox.com/melisseaires

I can always be found on Facebook. I run the fun Scifi Romance Group[2] and also Romancing the Shire[3]. My personal group is Melisse Aires' Lair[4]

BLOG: https://melisseaireswriter.wordpress.com/
Website: http://www.melisseairesbooks.weebly.com[5]
Facebook: https://www.facebook.com/melisseaires
IO News Group:https://groups.io/g/MelisseAiresPureEscapism

Please review if you enjoyed this romance!

---

2.   https://www.facebook.com/groups/the.scifi.romance.group/

3.   https://www.facebook.com/groups/romancingtheshire/

4.   https://www.facebook.com/groups/1732565730395151

5.   http://www.melisseairesbooks.com

Don't miss out!

Visit the website below and you can sign up to receive emails whenever Melisse Aires publishes a new book. There's no charge and no obligation.

https://books2read.com/r/B-A-PTK-SFRB

BOOKS 2 READ

Connecting independent readers to independent writers.

Also by Melisse Aires

Another Supernatural Apocalypse
Enchanted Bonds
Ritual of Fire and Ice

A Warm Winter Fantasy
Elf Wish
Christmas Wizardry
Faunication

Cyborg Nation
A Cyborg's Old Terran Christmas

Diaspora Worlds
Her Cyborg Awakes
Alien Blood
Starwoman's Sanctuary
Escaping Poison
Cyborg Security

Diaspora Worlds Bundle
Cyborg Liberation

Encanto Bay--Where Magic Happens
White Tiger Lover
The Psyvamp and the Professor
Holly Jolly Vampire
Single Mom, Vampire Lover

Far Stars Universe
Stranded on Grzbt
Christmas Cookies in Space
Pardblood, A Second Chance Romance

Love on the Space Frontier
Stars Between Us

Realms of Glister
Orc In Winter
Bridal Faire

Urloon
Refugees on Urloon